# Shadows Of Commerce - The Queen of Piracy

Smita Singh

Published by Smita Singh, 2024.

This is a work of fiction. Similarities to real people, places, or events are entirely coincidental.

SHADOWS OF COMMERCE - THE QUEEN OF PIRACY

**First edition. October 22, 2024.**

Copyright © 2024 Smita Singh.

ISBN: 979-8224780013

Written by Smita Singh.

# Shadows Of Commerce - The Queen of Piracy

In a world where everything seems to have a price, there exists a shadow industry that thrives on illusion. It's a world where brands are copied, products are imitated, and empires are built not on innovation, but on replication. The Queen of Piracy is a story about one woman's journey through this hidden economy, where profit trumps morality, and power is achieved at the expense of truth.

As I began writing this book, I was struck by how pervasive counterfeit products have become. From high-end luxury items to everyday essentials, the market is flooded with duplicates that challenge not only businesses, but consumers themselves. This story is inspired by the real-world complexities of this counterfeit industry, where deception isn't just a tactic—it's a way of life.

The Queen of Piracy is more than just a tale of ambition and greed. It's a reflection of how fragile success can be when it's built on shaky foundations. Through Elena Marcetti's rise and fall, we explore the hidden costs of seeking power in a world driven by imitation. Her story is a mirror to the times we live in—times where authenticity is often sacrificed for the allure of quick gains.

I hope that this story will not only entertain but also shed light on the ethical dilemmas faced by businesses and individuals in a world where counterfeit culture flourishes. As you delve into Elena's journey, you'll find a narrative that's both thrilling and thought-provoking, urging us all to question what we value in the products we consume and the people we admire.

Chapter 1: The Streets of Beginnings

Chapter 2: First Steps into Shadows

Chapter 3: The Turning Point

Chapter 4: Building the Machine

Chapter 5: The Art of Duplication

Chapter 6: A New Partner in the Game

Chapter 7: Shadows and Mirrors

Chapter 8: Whispers in the Dark

Chapter 9: Web of Intrigue

Chapter 10: New Territories, New Enemies

Chapter 11: A Powerful Ally Lost

Chapter 12: Cracks in the Empire

Chapter 13: The Media's Eye

Chapter 14: Scrambling for Control

Chapter 15: A House of Cards

Chapter 16: The Fall

**Chapter 17: Escape or Capture?**

**Chapter 18: The Aftermath**

**Chapter 19: Where is She?**

**Chapter 20: Legacy of Shadows**

# Chapter 1: The Streets of Beginnings

Elena Marcetti's life began in the crowded, bustling streets of her home city—an unremarkable neighbourhood where poverty blended seamlessly with the vibrant chaos of daily commerce. The narrow alleys were filled with vendors selling everything from fresh produce to imitation designer goods, all competing for the attention of passersby. The air was thick with the smells of fried street food, the sound of vendors shouting their bargains, and the hum of constant movement as people pushed through the markets. For as long as Elena could remember, this was the only life she knew.

Born into a struggling family, Elena's world was defined by survival. Her mother, Maria Marcetti, had a small stall tucked in one of the busiest sections of the market, where she sold knock-off handbags, shoes, and accessories to tourists and locals alike. Maria was a hardworking woman, but the business of counterfeit goods was unstable, and every day was a battle to sell enough to keep food on the table. Elena's father had left the family when she was just a baby, leaving Maria to raise her daughter alone, and the burden of keeping their heads above water weighed heavily on her.

Elena, even as a child, had always been sharp. She would often stand beside her mother at the stall, her curious eyes taking in the world around her. The stall wasn't glamorous—just a small wooden table with piles of fake designer goods carefully arranged to look enticing. Tourists would wander by, some pausing to admire the faux leather handbags with famous logos imprinted on them, while others moved on, uninterested. But young Elena had a knack for sensing which customers were willing to be persuaded, and she would often flash a smile at them, drawing them in with her innocent charm.

"Only 20 euros," Maria would say, holding up a handbag that looked like it had come from the glossy pages of a fashion magazine. "Looks just like the real thing."

More often than not, the customer would hesitate, but then, lured by the promise of a bargain, they would hand over the money. This dance between vendor and buyer fascinated Elena. She loved watching the way her mother negotiated, always keeping her voice light and her tone friendly, despite the struggles they faced. Elena quickly learned that it wasn't just the quality of the goods that mattered—though they were, admittedly, not great—but how you sold them. It was the illusion of value that made the sale.

Elena's fascination with the world of counterfeit goods began here, in the streets where imitation was a business and survival meant bending the rules. By the time she was eight years old, she knew the market like the back of her hand. She could spot which vendors were making decent profits and which ones were barely scraping by. She noticed which tourists were likely to fall for the charm of a knock-off handbag and which ones would scoff at the idea. And most of all, she learned that people, even those with money, loved a good bargain—even if it wasn't real.

Her mother had never hidden the truth from her about what they sold. She knew that the handbags, shoes, and watches on their stall were not genuine. They were imitations, copies made to look like expensive brands but sold at a fraction of the price. Yet, Elena never felt ashamed of this. To her, it wasn't just about selling fake products—it was about giving people something they wanted but couldn't afford. It was about finding a way to survive in a world that was far from fair.

"Elena, come here," Maria would call to her from behind the stall whenever a customer looked particularly interested in their goods. "Help me show this lady how lovely these handbags are."

Elena would rush over, her small hands gently picking up a bag and holding it up for the customer to see. She knew exactly what to say—Maria had taught her well. "It's just like the real one," she would say with a bright smile. "And you can get it for so much less!"

At first, Elena had simply mimicked her mother's words, not fully understanding the complexities of the market they operated in. But as she grew older, she began to see the larger picture. She saw how counterfeit goods were everywhere, not just in their stall, but in the other stalls nearby, in stores across the city, and even on people's backs as they walked down the street. It was an entire industry, built on imitating the unattainable and selling it to those who couldn't afford the real thing. And, to her surprise, it worked.

The more she observed, the more Elena's curiosity deepened. She began to ask questions—questions that her mother wasn't always able to answer. "Where do these handbags come from?" Elena asked one day as she helped her mother unpack a new shipment of goods.

Maria hesitated before responding. "They come from factories, sweetheart. Big factories that make these things and sell them to people like us so we can sell them in the markets."

"Are they bad?" Elena pressed. "For making fake things?"

Maria paused, her face clouded with uncertainty. She wasn't sure how to explain it to her young daughter. "It's not that simple, Elena," she finally said. "Some people might say it's wrong, but we're not hurting anyone. We're just trying to make a living. People buy these things because they want them, and we sell them because we need to survive."

Elena thought about her mother's words for a long time. She understood that life wasn't fair—after all, she had seen it with her own eyes. The rich people who walked through the market with their expensive clothes and real designer handbags didn't have to worry about where their next meal would come from. But for people like her and her mother, life was about doing what you could with what you had. And if that meant selling counterfeit goods, then so be it.

But Elena's fascination with the counterfeit world went beyond mere survival. As the years passed, she became more involved in the business, helping her mother at the stall every day after school. She learned how to haggle with customers, how to spot a potential buyer from a distance, and how to convince even the most sceptical of tourists that they were getting a great deal. She watched as her mother built relationships with the suppliers who brought them the goods—men who arrived in the middle of the night with boxes of knock-off products straight from factories across the border.

It wasn't long before Elena began to dream bigger. She loved the thrill of the market, the challenge of selling, and the satisfaction of knowing she had helped put food on the table. But she also saw the limitations of their small stall. She knew that as long as they stayed in the market, they would always be struggling. They would always be at the mercy of the suppliers, the vendors, and the tourists. And Elena wanted more than that.

By the time she was a teenager, Elena had developed a keen business sense. She began to question the system they operated in, wondering why they couldn't be the ones in charge. Why couldn't they be the ones who supplied the goods instead of relying on shady middlemen who took a large cut of the profits? Why couldn't they expand their business beyond the narrow streets of their city and into something larger?

One evening, after the market had closed and they were packing up the stall, Elena turned to her mother with a new determination in her eyes. "Mama, we should start our own business," she said, her voice filled with excitement.

Maria looked at her daughter, surprised by her boldness. "What do you mean? We already have a business, Elena."

"No, I mean a real business," Elena explained. "Not just selling here in the market. We could make our own products, sell them in other places, maybe even online. We don't have to rely on these middlemen anymore. We could do it ourselves."

Maria was silent for a moment, taken aback by her daughter's ambition. "That's a big dream, Elena. I'm not sure we have the money or the connections to do something like that."

Elena shook her head. "We'll find a way. I've been thinking about it, and I know we can do it. People love these products. They're willing to buy them, even if they know they're fake. Imagine if we could make our own versions, ones that look even better than the ones we're selling now. We could start small and build up from there."

Her mother smiled, both proud and worried. She had always known that Elena was special—that she had a mind for business far beyond her years. But she also knew how difficult the world could be, and she didn't want her daughter to get hurt by chasing impossible dreams.

Still, there was something in Elena's eyes that gave Maria hope. Perhaps, just perhaps, her daughter could achieve something greater than the life they had been living. After all, the market had taught them both one valuable lesson: in this world, nothing was impossible if you were willing to take risks.

From that moment on, Elena's mind was set. She would not be content to sell knock-offs for the rest of her life. She saw a world of opportunity beyond the narrow streets of her home city, and she was determined to find her way there.

The streets of beginnings had taught her how to survive, but they had also ignited a spark in her—a desire to escape the confines of poverty and build something bigger. The counterfeit goods that had once been a means of survival were now, in Elena's eyes, a stepping stone to something much greater. And as she stood in the market that day, watching the crowds pass by, she knew that her journey was just beginning.

In the years that followed, Elena would grow from a curious child selling knock-off handbags to a savvy businesswoman with grand ambitions. But the path ahead would be anything but easy, and the world of counterfeit goods was far more complex and dangerous than she could have ever imagined.

# Chapter 2: First Steps into Shadows

Elena Marcetti was no longer the curious child weaving her way through the crowded market stalls, helping her mother sell counterfeit goods to tourists. Now a young adult, she stood at the brink of a new chapter in her life. The market had taught her invaluable lessons about survival, negotiation, and the art of selling an illusion. But Elena had always wanted more. The small-time hustle of selling knock-off handbags and shoes on the streets wasn't enough to satisfy her growing ambition. She wanted to break free from the market's limitations and build something that was truly her own.

Her first step into the world beyond the crowded stalls wasn't as easy as she had imagined. While her mother continued running the family stall, Elena began venturing out on her own, seeking new opportunities. She no longer wanted to be a mere vendor—she wanted to control the supply. She dreamed of creating a business where she didn't have to rely on middlemen, where the products she sold were her own, even if they weren't genuine. But to do that, she had to start small. She needed to build connections, understand the supply chain, and, most importantly, learn the craft of making counterfeit goods that were nearly indistinguishable from the originals.

Elena's first real contact in the world of underground counterfeit trade came from a chance meeting. It was late one evening when she was closing up her mother's stall. A man had approached her, a slim figure with sharp eyes that darted around the market, scanning the scene with the precision of someone who didn't want to be noticed. He wore a worn leather jacket and had the kind of face that seemed to blend into the crowd, but his voice was calm and confident as he spoke.

"You sell good stuff," he said, his eyes falling on the last handbag Elena was packing away.

Elena glanced at him cautiously. She had learned to be wary of strangers—especially those who appeared too interested in their products. "Just doing what we can to make a living," she replied, her tone neutral.

The man chuckled softly, stepping closer. "I can see you've got potential, though. You're not like the other vendors here."

Something about his words made Elena pause. She wasn't sure whether it was a compliment or a subtle threat, but she could sense that this man wasn't just another tourist or local shopper. There was something more to him—something that suggested he knew more about the world of counterfeit goods than he was letting on.

"What do you mean?" she asked, folding her arms.

He smiled. "I mean, you've got the eye. You know what sells, what people want. But this"—he gestured to the handbags on the table—"this is small-time. If you want to make real money, you need better connections. You need to be smarter about where you get your goods."

Elena felt a surge of curiosity. She had spent years thinking about how she could expand beyond the market, but this was the first time someone had openly acknowledged her ambitions. "And you know where I can find those connections?" she asked, trying to sound casual.

The man nodded, his smile widening. "Maybe. But first, I need to know if you're serious about this. This isn't a game, kid. The people I deal with don't take kindly to amateurs or time-wasters."

Elena felt a flicker of excitement mixed with caution. She knew she was venturing into dangerous territory, but the promise of something bigger, something more profitable, was too tempting to resist. She had spent years watching others succeed while her family struggled to get by. Now, she wanted a chance to prove that she could do more than just survive—she could thrive.

"I'm serious," she said, her voice steady.

The man nodded again, satisfied with her response. "Meet me tomorrow at the old warehouse by the docks. Midnight. And come alone."

With that, he turned and disappeared into the crowd, leaving Elena standing by the stall, her heart racing. She didn't know what to expect, but she knew that this was the opportunity she had been waiting for. It was time to take her first steps into the shadows of the counterfeit world—a world that promised both danger and fortune.

The next night, Elena made her way to the old warehouse by the docks, her mind filled with a mix of excitement and fear. She had told her mother that she would be out late, helping a friend, and Maria hadn't questioned her. In truth, Elena hadn't wanted to explain where she was really going or why. Her mother had always been cautious when it came to dealing with new suppliers, preferring to stick with the ones she trusted. But Elena knew that playing it safe would only keep them trapped in the same cycle of poverty.

The warehouse was as old and decrepit as she had imagined. The large, rusted doors creaked as she pushed them open, and the dim light inside barely illuminated the cavernous space. Crates were stacked high along the walls, and the air smelled of saltwater and dust. She could hear the distant sound of the ocean waves crashing against the docks outside.

As she stepped further inside, the man from the market emerged from the shadows. He was not alone. Two other men stood beside him, both watching her closely. One was tall and broad-shouldered, his arms crossed over his chest, while the other was shorter and leaner, his eyes sharp and calculating.

"Good to see you made it," the man said, his voice echoing in the empty warehouse.

Elena nodded, trying to keep her composure. "I said I was serious, didn't I?"

He smirked. "You did. Now, let's get down to business."

He motioned to the tall man, who stepped forward and opened one of the crates. Inside were dozens of handbags—just like the ones Elena had been selling at the market. But as she looked closer, she realized something was different. These bags weren't the cheap knock-offs she was used to seeing. They were almost perfect replicas—so close to the real thing that it was hard to tell the difference.

"These," the man said, gesturing to the crate, "are some of the finest counterfeit goods you'll find anywhere. Made in a factory just across the border. The materials are better, the craftsmanship is top-notch, and they sell for twice the price of the ones you're used to."

Elena was impressed. She had never seen counterfeit goods of such high quality before. "How much are you selling them for?" she asked, her mind already racing with possibilities.

The man smiled. "That's where the deal comes in. You sell these for 100 euros a piece, and we'll give you a cut of 30 percent. You keep the rest."

Elena did the quick math in her head. That was a significant increase from what she had been making at the market. "And what's the catch?" she asked, knowing that there was always a catch in deals like this.

The man's smile faded slightly. "The catch is that you have to sell them quietly. No attracting attention. The authorities don't like it when people start selling high-quality fakes, especially not ones this convincing. You'll have to keep your head down, stick to the people you trust, and make sure no one rats you out."

Elena nodded slowly. She understood the risks. Selling counterfeit goods was illegal, and the better the quality, the more likely it was to attract unwanted attention. But she also knew that this was her chance to break into a larger, more lucrative market. If she could pull it off, she could finally start building the business she had always dreamed of.

"I can do it," she said, her voice filled with determination.

The man seemed pleased with her response. "Good. We'll give you a small batch to start with. If you can move them quickly and without any trouble, we'll talk about expanding."

Over the next few weeks, Elena threw herself into her new venture with everything she had. She started selling the high-quality fakes to her trusted customers—people who had been buying from her mother's stall for years and knew how to keep quiet. The bags sold like hotcakes. Word spread quickly among the locals that Elena had access to the best counterfeit goods in the city, and soon, she had a growing list of clients eager to buy from her.

But as her success grew, so did her ambitions. Elena began reaching out to new suppliers, forming relationships with people who could provide her with not just handbags, but shoes, watches, and even electronics. She learned the ins and outs of the counterfeit trade—how to source materials, how to negotiate prices, and most importantly, how to avoid getting caught.

One of her most important lessons came from a man named Luca, a veteran in the world of counterfeit goods. Luca had been in the business for decades, and he had seen it all—raids, arrests, and double-crosses. He took an immediate liking to Elena, impressed by her drive and intelligence.

"You've got potential, kid," he told her one evening as they sat in a dimly lit bar, discussing a potential deal for counterfeit watches. "But you need to be careful. This business can chew you up and spit you out if you're not smart."

Elena nodded, taking his advice to heart. She had always known that the world she was stepping into was dangerous, but Luca's words made it clear just how high the stakes were. The counterfeit trade was a shadowy world, filled with people who would do anything to protect their profits.

Still, Elena was determined. She wasn't afraid of taking risks—she had been doing that her whole life. And as her network of suppliers grew, so did her confidence. She began to see herself not just as a vendor, but as a player in a much larger game. She was no longer content to sell other people's products—she wanted to create her own.

By the time Elena turned twenty-one, she had built a small but profitable operation. She had suppliers, customers, and a growing reputation in the underground world of counterfeit goods. But she wasn't satisfied yet. She knew that if she wanted to become truly successful, she would have to expand even further. She wanted to move beyond the shadows and into the world of big business.

And so, with the same determination that had driven her since childhood, Elena took her first real steps toward building her empire.

# Chapter 3: The Turning Point

Elena Marcetti had tasted success in the underground world of counterfeit goods, but she knew that her small operation was only the beginning. With her sharp mind and growing network of suppliers, she had built a reputation in her city for selling some of the finest counterfeit handbags and shoes. But even as her profits grew, so did her ambitions. Elena was no longer content with local sales; she wanted to expand her reach beyond the narrow streets of her home city. She wanted to take her business to an international level.

The opportunity came in the form of a man named Viktor Koval. Elena first heard his name whispered among the seasoned counterfeit traders she had started to deal with. Viktor was an international dealer in counterfeit electronics—smartphones, tablets, computers, and even home appliances. His business operated on a scale far larger than anything Elena had ever imagined. He supplied goods to markets across Europe, Asia, and even parts of North America. While Elena had dabbled in the world of high-quality fake designer goods, electronics were an entirely different beast. Counterfeit electronics promised bigger profits, but they also came with greater risks.

One evening, while discussing potential deals with Luca, her mentor in the underground world of counterfeits, Elena casually mentioned that she was thinking of expanding beyond fashion.

Luca raised an eyebrow. "Fashion's safe, Elena. People buy knock-off handbags because they're status symbols. Electronics, though—that's a different game."

Elena was unfazed. "Bigger profits, though."

Luca leaned back in his chair, his sharp eyes never leaving hers. "Yeah, but bigger problems, too. Fake electronics can be dangerous.

Defective batteries, faulty wiring. One bad product, and you're dealing with lawsuits, recalls, maybe even criminal charges."

Elena crossed her arms, her mind already made up. "I've been hearing about a guy—Viktor Koval. People say he's a ghost, but he runs one of the biggest counterfeit electronics operations in the world. I want to meet him."

Luca sighed. "Of course you do. You never do things halfway." He paused for a moment, clearly weighing his next words carefully. "I can put in a word for you, but don't think for a second that Viktor's going to be easy to impress. He deals with serious players. You're just getting started, kid."

Elena smiled. "You said I have potential, didn't you?"

A week later, Elena received a message from Luca. "Midnight. The shipping yard by the old pier. Come alone."

Elena knew what this meant. It was time to meet Viktor. She prepared herself as best she could, mentally rehearsing what she would say, how she would present herself. She had worked too hard to miss this opportunity. A contact like Viktor could change everything for her—open doors to new markets, bigger profits, and the kind of power she had always dreamed of.

The night was cold, the salty breeze from the nearby ocean chilling her as she made her way to the shipping yard. The area was deserted except for the distant hum of cargo ships and the occasional rumble of a truck moving containers. The air smelled of rust and seaweed. She kept her head down, her hands deep in her coat pockets, as she walked through the narrow maze of containers until she reached the meeting point.

Viktor Koval was already there, standing in the shadows next to a black SUV. He was taller than she had expected, with a stocky build and a clean-shaven face. His icy blue eyes watched her as she approached, giving nothing away. Two men stood on either side of him, their expressions unreadable.

"You must be Elena Marcetti," Viktor said, his voice calm and measured, with a hint of an Eastern European accent. "Luca speaks highly of you."

Elena felt a surge of confidence. She had come prepared, and she was determined to show Viktor that she was more than just another small-time vendor. "I hear you're the man to talk to if I want to expand."

Viktor raised an eyebrow, his expression unreadable. "Expand into what?"

"Electronics," Elena replied without hesitation. "I've been successful with fashion, but I want to take the next step. I've heard you deal in large-scale operations, international supply chains. That's what I want to learn."

For a moment, Viktor said nothing, his eyes studying her. Elena could feel the weight of his gaze, and she forced herself to hold her ground. Finally, he nodded slowly. "You're ambitious. That's good. But ambition without caution is dangerous in this business."

Elena smiled, a small, determined smile. "I'm cautious. And I'm ready."

Viktor turned to one of the men beside him and gave a slight nod. The man stepped forward, handing Elena a tablet. On the screen were detailed images of various counterfeit electronics—smartphones, tablets, gaming consoles. They looked almost identical to the real thing, down to the logos and packaging.

"These," Viktor said, "are some of our best-selling products. High-quality replicas, made in factories across China, Eastern Europe, and parts of Southeast Asia. They sell for a fraction of the price of the real thing, and most buyers can't tell the difference. But this is not a small-time operation, Elena. We're talking about shipping containers full of goods, distributed to multiple countries. It's risky, and it requires careful planning. One mistake, and you're not just losing money—you're facing international law enforcement."

Elena studied the images carefully. She knew that this was her chance to prove herself. "I can handle it," she said. "I've been running my own operation for years now, and I know how to keep things quiet. Give me a chance, and I'll show you that I'm ready for more."

Viktor nodded, seemingly satisfied with her response. "Very well. We'll start with a small shipment—fifty smartphones. You'll sell them locally and report back on how it goes. If you're successful, we'll talk about expanding."

Over the next few weeks, Elena found herself diving deeper into the counterfeit world than she ever had before. Viktor's shipment of smartphones arrived without incident, and Elena quickly realized just how lucrative the electronics market could be. The phones were high-quality replicas, and buyers were eager to get their hands on them at a fraction of the price of the real thing. Word spread quickly, and soon Elena had a list of clients willing to pay top dollar for the fake electronics.

As her success grew, so did her network. Viktor introduced her to suppliers across the world—factories in China that specialized in producing counterfeit electronics, shipping companies that knew how to smuggle goods across borders undetected, and distributors in major cities who could move the products quickly and quietly. Elena had always been good at networking, but now she was playing on a global scale. She was no longer just a vendor in a crowded market—she was a businesswoman, operating in the shadows of international trade.

With each new shipment, Elena's profits grew. She used the money to expand her operation, hiring a small team of trusted individuals to help with distribution and logistics. She learned the ins and outs of international supply chains—how to source materials, how to negotiate prices, and how to avoid detection by authorities. It was a delicate balancing act, but Elena thrived in the high-stakes environment. She had always been resourceful, and now, she had the resources to back up her ambitions.

But success came with its own set of challenges. The bigger her operation grew, the more attention it attracted. Elena knew that she had to be careful—one wrong move, and everything she had built could come crashing down. She took precautions, using false identities and offshore accounts to cover her tracks. She learned how to move money discreetly, funneling her profits through a network of shell companies and shady accountants. It was a dangerous game, but Elena was determined to win.

Her relationship with Viktor also deepened. The two of them met regularly to discuss business, and Elena found herself learning more from him than she had ever anticipated. Viktor was a master of the counterfeit trade, with decades of experience and a network of contacts that spanned the globe. He taught her how to navigate the complexities of international markets, how to deal with corrupt officials, and how to spot potential threats before they became problems.

"You're doing well, Elena," Viktor said during one of their meetings. "But remember, this business is built on trust. You need to know who your allies are, and who might betray you. One misstep, and everything you've built can be taken away in an instant."

Elena nodded, taking his words to heart. She had always known that the counterfeit world was dangerous, but now, more than ever, she understood just how high the stakes were. She had come too far to lose everything now.

As the months passed, Elena's operation continued to grow. She expanded beyond smartphones, moving into other areas of counterfeit electronics—tablets, gaming consoles, even home appliances. Her business was booming, and she was making more money than she had ever dreamed possible. But with success came increased scrutiny. Law enforcement agencies across Europe were cracking down on counterfeit goods, and Elena knew that it was only a matter of time before they turned their attention to her.

But Elena was prepared. She had built a web of connections that spanned multiple countries, and she knew how to stay one step ahead of the authorities. She operated in the shadows, always careful to cover her tracks and avoid detection. And yet, she couldn't shake the feeling that she was being watched—that her every move was being monitored.

The turning point in Elena's career had come, and she had embraced it fully. But as she ventured deeper into the world of counterfeit goods, she knew that the road ahead would only become more treacherous. She had built an empire, but now she had to protect it at all costs.

# Chapter 4: Building the Machine

Elena Marcetti had taken the first major steps into the world of high-stakes counterfeiting by establishing herself as a trusted player in the international electronics black market. Her relationship with Viktor Koval had opened doors she never thought possible, and she was growing her empire faster than ever. However, Elena was far from satisfied. She wasn't content with merely reselling goods produced by others. She wanted more control, more power, and most importantly, more profit. The logical next step for her was to establish her own counterfeit manufacturing operation. This would eliminate the need for middlemen and allow her to scale her business to new heights.

Elena understood that starting her own production line was a risky venture. It wasn't like selling handbags on the street corner—manufacturing counterfeit goods required capital, machinery, labor, and, most importantly, secrecy. But Elena thrived on challenges, and she knew that this was the path to true success. If she could control the entire process—from production to distribution—she would become unstoppable.

**The first hurdle was finding a location where she could set up her operation. It needed to be remote, far away from the prying eyes of law enforcement or competitors, but close enough to major trade routes to ensure smooth distribution. Elena knew she couldn't rely on public factories, which would be far too exposed. She needed to find places that were off the grid, in countries with weak enforcement of intellectual property laws and a high tolerance for corruption.**

Elena called on Viktor's contacts for advice. One of them, a middleman based in Eastern Europe named Ivan, suggested a series of abandoned factories in Moldova and rural parts of Ukraine. These locations had been shut down after the collapse of the Soviet Union, but they still had the basic infrastructure needed for large-scale manufacturing. More importantly, the local governments were notoriously corrupt, and Elena knew that a few well-placed bribes would buy her the freedom to operate without too many questions.

Armed with this information, Elena flew to Moldova under the guise of a businesswoman looking for real estate investments. She had learned to blend in well, adopting the appearance of a legitimate entrepreneur while carefully concealing her true intentions. Accompanied by one of Ivan's trusted associates, Elena toured several old factories, their walls crumbling and machinery rusted from years of neglect. Despite their dilapidated condition, Elena could see the potential.

One factory, in particular, caught her eye. It was located in a small village far from the nearest city, surrounded by thick forests and farmlands. The village itself had fallen on hard times—its economy decimated after the fall of the Soviet Union, leaving many of its residents unemployed and struggling to make ends meet. To Elena, this meant one thing: cheap labor.

She smiled as she walked through the factory's dusty halls. The roof needed repairs, the equipment needed updating, and the place would require significant investment to get it up and running, but none of that deterred her. She could already see it in her mind—a state-of-the-art facility, churning out counterfeit electronics, clothing, and more. It was the first piece of the puzzle, and she knew it was the perfect place to begin.

Elena wasted no time in putting her plan into action. Once she had secured the factory, her next step was to hire workers. She needed people who wouldn't ask too many questions—locals who were desperate for work and willing to keep their heads down. Elena knew from experience that loyalty could be bought with the right incentives, and in this village, money spoke louder than words.

She recruited a local fixer named Andrei to help her. Andrei had deep connections in the village and knew who to talk to in order to get things done. Together, they began recruiting workers, offering wages that, while modest by Western standards, were more than generous in this impoverished part of the world.

At first, the workers were hesitant. They had heard rumors about Elena's business, and while many of them were desperate for work, they weren't sure if they wanted to be involved in something illegal. But Elena had a gift for persuasion. She spoke to the workers directly, assuring them that they wouldn't be in any danger. Her operation was sophisticated, she explained, and she had powerful friends who would protect them. Besides, the work was easy—assembling products, packaging them, and shipping them out. There was nothing violent or dangerous about it.

Andrei backed her up, spreading word around the village that Elena was a generous employer who took care of her people. Slowly, the workers began to sign on. Most of them were men and women who had lost their jobs when the old factories shut down, and they were grateful for the opportunity to earn a living again. For them, this was just another job—one that paid well and offered some sense of stability.

Elena also made sure to bring in a few key specialists—engineers who could help upgrade the machinery and technicians who could oversee quality control. These were the people who would ensure that her products were nearly indistinguishable from the real thing. She knew that in the world of counterfeits, quality was everything. If her goods were too obvious as fakes, they would be worthless. But if she could produce high-quality replicas, she could charge premium prices and attract more discerning buyers.

Once the factory was operational, Elena's next challenge was perfecting the art of counterfeiting. She had already learned a great deal from her time working with Viktor, but now that she was in control of her own production, she needed to take her skills to the next level. This wasn't about selling cheap knock-offs anymore—Elena wanted to produce goods that could pass for the real thing, whether they were electronics, designer clothing, or luxury goods.

To achieve this, she hired experts in reverse engineering. These were people who had worked in legitimate factories before, and they knew how to take a real product and break it down to its most basic components. Once they had analyzed the original, they could replicate it almost perfectly, using cheaper materials and slightly altered designs to cut costs while maintaining the appearance of authenticity.

Elena spent hours in the factory, overseeing the production process, testing products herself, and pushing her workers to improve their methods. She wasn't just running a business—she was building an empire, and she wanted every detail to be perfect.

One of her first major successes came in the form of counterfeit smartphones. Elena had secured a shipment of real phones from a legitimate dealer, and her engineers worked tirelessly to recreate them. They used lower-grade screens, cheaper processors, and cut corners wherever possible, but the final product looked almost identical to the original. When Elena held the first finished phone in her hands, she couldn't help but smile. It was a thing of beauty—a high-quality fake that could be sold for a fraction of the price of the real thing, but with a much higher profit margin.

She knew that she had struck gold.

As Elena's operation grew, she realized that she couldn't rely on her network of suppliers and distributors alone. To protect her business and ensure its continued success, she needed to form alliances with powerful people who could offer her protection. This meant forging relationships with corrupt politicians, law enforcement officials, and business leaders who had a vested interest in seeing her operation succeed.

Elena's entry into this world was facilitated by Viktor, who introduced her to several key figures in Eastern Europe's political and business circles. One of these men was Mikhail Petrov, a high-ranking politician in Moldova with deep connections to the country's ruling party. Mikhail had been involved in shady deals for years, and he saw Elena's operation as an opportunity to expand his own influence.

Over a series of discreet meetings in expensive restaurants and private clubs, Elena and Mikhail reached an understanding. In exchange for a cut of her profits, Mikhail would use his political power to shield her business from scrutiny. He would make sure that local law enforcement turned a blind eye to her factories, and he would smooth over any bureaucratic obstacles that arose. In return, Elena would keep her operation running smoothly, providing him with a steady stream of income.

It was a mutually beneficial arrangement, and one that allowed Elena to operate with near impunity. She knew that as long as she had Mikhail and others like him in her corner, she could continue expanding her empire without fear of interference.

With her factory up and running and her political connections in place, Elena turned her attention to expanding her distribution network. She already had a foothold in the local market, but she knew that the real money was in international sales. To achieve this, she needed to establish new shipping routes, forge partnerships with overseas distributors, and bribe customs officials to ensure that her goods could move freely across borders.

Elena traveled frequently during this period, meeting with potential business partners in countries as far-flung as China, India, and Turkey. These were places where counterfeit goods were in high demand, and where enforcement of intellectual property laws was often lax. She built a web of contacts—smugglers, corrupt customs officials, and underground dealers—who helped her move her products across borders and into the hands of buyers.

Each new market brought new challenges, but Elena thrived on the complexity of it all. She loved the thrill of negotiating deals in smoke-filled backrooms, the satisfaction of seeing her goods sold in markets thousands of miles away, and the knowledge that she was outsmarting the system at every turn.

By the time Elena's factories were fully operational, her counterfeit empire was no longer a small-time operation. She had built a sophisticated network that spanned multiple countries, employing hundreds of workers and producing thousands of counterfeit products every month. Her goods were being sold in markets across Europe, Asia, and the Middle East, and her profits were soaring.

Elena had become a queen in her own right—a queen of the counterfeit world. But even as her empire grew, she knew that she couldn't rest on her laurels. There were always new challenges to face, new competitors to outmaneuver, and new markets to conquer.

And deep down, Elena knew that the road ahead would only become more dangerous. The more powerful she became, the more enemies she would make. But for now, she reveled in her success, knowing that she had built something extraordinary.

The machine was running, and Elena was at the helm.

# Chapter 5: The Art of Duplication

By the time Elena Marcetti had fully established her counterfeit empire, she was no longer just the street-smart girl who sold knock-off handbags to tourists. She had become a master of duplication, replicating everything from high-end electronics to designer fashion with a precision that fooled even the most discerning buyers. Her operations had reached a scale that few could have imagined, and Elena had only just begun.

Now, with her counterfeit factories humming at full capacity, Elena set her sights on new industries. She wasn't content with simply producing electronics and clothing anymore—she wanted to dominate entire markets. Her ambition grew alongside her empire, and she knew that the key to staying ahead of her competitors was diversification. She needed to expand into other industries, create new lines of counterfeit products, and flood global markets with goods that would be impossible to distinguish from the originals.

The world of duplication was not just about making copies—it was about mastering the fine details that made fakes indistinguishable from the real thing. Elena knew that this was an art form, and she was determined to become its greatest artist.

**Elena's first move into a new industry came when she decided to target the luxury fashion market. High-end designer goods had always been a lucrative business, but counterfeiting these products required a different level of expertise. The world of fashion was all about exclusivity, and customers who bought luxury items prided themselves on owning something rare and unique. The challenge, therefore, was not just to replicate the appearance of designer items, but to recreate their craftsmanship.**

To begin her foray into luxury fashion, Elena hired a team of skilled artisans from Italy and France, many of whom had worked for legitimate fashion houses before falling on hard times. These artisans had the knowledge and experience to replicate even the most intricate details of high-end products. They could produce leather goods with perfect stitching, handbags with signature hardware, and clothes that mimicked the fabric and fit of the original designs.

Elena also sourced high-quality materials, knowing that this was crucial to creating believable fakes. She imported leather from the same suppliers that sold to luxury brands and used the same factories that produced authentic zippers, buttons, and accessories. Her goal was to create products so perfect that even an expert would struggle to tell them apart from the originals.

Her first major success came with a line of counterfeit handbags. These were replicas of some of the most sought-after designs in the world—bags that sold for thousands of dollars in upscale boutiques. Elena's versions, however, were priced at a fraction of the cost, but looked and felt just like the real thing. She made sure that her products were distributed through underground channels that catered to wealthy clients who wanted luxury goods but were unwilling to pay full price.

Within months, Elena's counterfeit handbags were appearing in markets across Europe, Asia, and the Middle East. They were sold in backroom shops, online marketplaces, and even high-end boutiques that unknowingly stocked her fakes. Many buyers believed they were getting a deal on an authentic product, never realizing that they were holding a counterfeit in their hands.

Elena's success in the fashion industry was a testament to her ability to adapt and innovate. She had mastered the art of duplication, and her products were indistinguishable from the originals in every way that mattered.

After conquering the luxury fashion market, Elena turned her attention back to electronics. She had already established herself as a major player in the counterfeit electronics industry, but she wanted more. The demand for high-end gadgets was growing rapidly, and Elena saw an opportunity to expand her product offerings beyond smartphones.

One of her first targets was the booming market for wearable technology. Smartwatches, fitness trackers, and wireless earbuds had become popular status symbols, and consumers were willing to pay top dollar for the latest models. Elena knew that if she could produce convincing replicas of these products, she could tap into a massive new market.

Once again, she assembled a team of engineers and technicians to reverse-engineer the most popular wearable devices on the market. These experts broke down the original products, analyzing every component and figuring out how to replicate them using cheaper materials. It was a painstaking process, but one that Elena insisted on. She knew that quality was key, and her customers wouldn't settle for anything less than perfection.

The result was a line of counterfeit smartwatches and fitness trackers that looked identical to the originals. They had the same sleek designs, the same features, and even the same logos. Elena's team had gone so far as to replicate the user interface of the original devices, making it nearly impossible to tell that they were fakes.

These products flooded the market, and Elena's distribution network made sure they reached customers all over the world. From street markets in Southeast Asia to online platforms in Europe, her counterfeit electronics were selling faster than she could produce them. And because they were so convincing, many buyers never even questioned their authenticity.

With her success in fashion and electronics, Elena's confidence grew, and she began to consider even riskier ventures. One of the most lucrative industries in the world was pharmaceuticals, and the demand for prescription drugs was constantly rising. But counterfeiting pharmaceuticals was a dangerous business. Unlike handbags or gadgets, fake drugs could have serious consequences for the people who used them. If something went wrong, it could mean lawsuits, criminal charges, or worse.

But Elena was undeterred. She knew that there was a huge black market for prescription drugs, especially in developing countries where access to legitimate medicines was limited. If she could produce counterfeit versions of popular drugs, she could make a fortune.

Elena started by targeting generic medications—drugs that were already being produced by multiple manufacturers and were widely available. These were easier to replicate, and the risk of detection was lower. She hired chemists who had worked in the pharmaceutical industry and tasked them with developing formulas that mimicked the real drugs.

Once her chemists had perfected the formulas, Elena set up small-scale production labs in several countries. These labs operated in secret, hidden in industrial areas or rural villages where they were unlikely to attract attention. The drugs they produced were packaged in bottles and blister packs that looked identical to those used by legitimate pharmaceutical companies, complete with fake labels and serial numbers.

Elena's counterfeit drugs were sold through underground pharmacies and online platforms, where buyers were often unaware that they were purchasing fakes. The drugs were cheaper than the real thing, and in many cases, they worked well enough to satisfy customers. But Elena knew that she was playing a dangerous game.

If any of her counterfeit drugs caused harm, it could bring her entire operation crashing down.

Despite the risks, Elena continued to expand her pharmaceutical business, always careful to stay one step ahead of the authorities. She was making millions from her fake medications, and she wasn't about to stop.

Elena's ambition didn't stop at fashion, electronics, or pharmaceuticals. She wanted to break into industries that no one had thought possible for counterfeiters. One of those industries was automotive parts.

The global automotive industry was worth billions, and there was a constant demand for replacement parts. From brake pads to engine components, the market for auto parts was vast and varied. Elena knew that if she could produce counterfeit parts that were good enough to pass as genuine, she could tap into a new source of revenue.

But counterfeiting automotive parts presented unique challenges. Unlike handbags or electronics, which could be easily replicated with cheaper materials, auto parts had to meet strict safety and performance standards. A faulty brake pad or engine part could lead to accidents, lawsuits, and even deaths. Elena knew she couldn't afford to cut corners if she wanted to succeed in this market.

To solve this problem, she brought in a team of mechanical engineers and automotive experts who had experience working in legitimate factories. These experts helped her source materials and design parts that would meet safety standards while still being cost-effective to produce. They also worked closely with her factories to ensure that the manufacturing process was as precise as possible.

Elena's first venture into the automotive industry was a line of counterfeit brake pads. These pads were designed to look and perform just like the originals, and they were sold to distributors who supplied repair shops and auto parts retailers. The pads were cheaper than the genuine parts, but they were good enough to pass inspections and keep customers happy.

As her automotive business grew, Elena expanded her product line to include other parts—engine components, transmission parts, and even tires. Each new product brought new challenges, but Elena thrived on the complexity of it all. She loved the thrill of mastering new industries and proving that her counterfeit empire could succeed in any market.

As Elena's empire grew, so did the scope of her clientele. Initially, her counterfeit products had been sold to middle-class consumers who were looking for deals on luxury goods or gadgets. But as her reputation for quality spread, her products began to reach even the wealthiest clients.

In the world of high fashion and luxury goods, exclusivity was everything. But even the wealthiest buyers couldn't resist a good deal. Elena's counterfeit handbags, watches, and clothing were so convincing that they began to find their way into the wardrobes of the rich and famous. Celebrities, socialites, and even business tycoons unknowingly purchased her fakes, believing they were getting authentic products at a fraction of the price.

Elena's success in reaching this elite clientele was a testament to the quality of her products. She had perfected the art of duplication to such an extent that her counterfeits were indistinguishable from the real thing. Her customers, whether they were buying a $10,000 handbag or a $50,000 watch, never suspected that they were being deceived.

By the time Elena's empire was in full swing, her products had flooded markets across the globe. From street vendors in Bangkok to upscale boutiques in Milan, her counterfeits were everywhere. Her factories were running day and night, churning out thousands of products that were sold in dozens of countries.

Elena had become a global player in the counterfeit industry, and her reach extended to every corner of the world. She had connections with suppliers, distributors, and corrupt officials in countries across Europe, Asia, and the Middle East. Her counterfeit goods were sold in markets both legitimate and underground, and her profits were soaring.

But with success came new challenges. As her empire grew, so did the attention from law enforcement and rival counterfeiters. Elena knew that staying ahead of the game would require constant vigilance and innovation.

Elena Marcetti had mastered the art of duplication, building an empire that spanned industries and continents. But even as she basked in her success, she knew that the world of counterfeiting was a dangerous one. The stakes were higher than ever, and the risks were growing. Yet for Elena, the thrill of the game was irresistible.

*The art of duplication was not just a business—it was her life.*

# Chapter 6: A New Partner in the Game

Elena Marcetti had built her counterfeit empire on a foundation of precision, innovation, and ruthless ambition. She had mastered the art of duplication, creating high-quality fakes that flooded global markets and penetrated industries as varied as fashion, electronics, pharmaceuticals, and automotive parts. Her operation was vast, her network extensive, and her profits immense. But as her empire grew, so did the risks. She was no longer just an underground player, unnoticed by the authorities—her success had made her a target.

It was only a matter of time before the law would catch up with her. Or so it seemed.

One day, while reviewing reports of an upcoming crackdown on counterfeit goods in one of her key markets, Elena realized she needed more than just money and influence to protect her empire. She needed a shield—someone powerful enough to protect her operations from government agencies, law enforcement, and regulatory bodies. This was a game of survival, and Elena knew it was time to take things to the next level.

That's when she met Mario Costa, a rising star in the world of politics. He was young, ambitious, and as ruthless as Elena. And most importantly, he was looking for the kind of financial backing that could turn his political career into an unstoppable force. Elena saw in him the opportunity she needed—a new partner in the game.

**The introduction came through one of Elena's trusted intermediaries, a middleman who had connections in both the business world and the political sphere. His name was Lorenzo, and he had long been Elena's go-to person for making discreet arrangements. One evening, as they sat in a quiet, upscale restaurant far from the public eye, Lorenzo introduced the idea of meeting Mario Costa.**

"Elena, there's someone you should meet," Lorenzo said, his tone casual but carrying an undertone of significance. "He's young, he's ambitious, and he's hungry for power. He's also got a good shot at winning the next election in one of your key markets. And I have a feeling that you two could... help each other."

Elena leaned back in her chair, her eyes narrowing slightly as she considered Lorenzo's words. She was always wary of politicians—they could be unpredictable and self-serving, traits she usually despised. But she trusted Lorenzo, and she knew that if he was suggesting this, it wasn't without careful thought.

"Tell me more," she said, intrigued but cautious.

Lorenzo smiled, sensing her interest. "Mario Costa is running for governor in a region that's critical to your operations. If he wins, he'll have the power to control the local police, the regulatory bodies, and even some of the national agencies that could be a threat to your business. He's ambitious, but he needs funding—substantial funding—for his campaign. That's where you come in."

Elena raised an eyebrow, intrigued. She had funded political candidates before, but this felt different. This was bigger, riskier, and far more important to the future of her empire.

"And what does he want in return?" Elena asked.

"Protection," Lorenzo replied. "He wants to rise to power, and he needs financial support to get there. In return, he can ensure that your operations remain untouched by the authorities. He'll provide cover for you—make sure that your factories, your shipments, your distribution networks are off-limits to law enforcement. Essentially, he'll make you untouchable."

Elena considered this for a moment. The idea was tempting, but it also carried risks. If Costa lost, or if he turned on her, it could expose her entire operation. But if he won—if he became governor—then she would have the kind of protection she had only dreamed of.

"I'll meet him," Elena finally said. "But I'll decide after I get a sense of who he is."

The meeting with Mario Costa was arranged for a private estate on the outskirts of the city. It was late at night, the kind of clandestine meeting that felt straight out of a spy novel. Elena arrived in a sleek black car, flanked by her security detail. She had learned long ago to be cautious—especially when dealing with people as ambitious as Costa.

Inside, she found Costa waiting for her, seated in a lavish drawing room adorned with expensive art and leather furniture. He stood as she entered, extending his hand with a charming smile that seemed a little too perfect.

"Ms. Marcetti," he said smoothly. "It's an honor to finally meet you."

Elena smiled politely, but her eyes remained cool. She studied Costa carefully, sizing him up. He was younger than she had expected, perhaps in his mid-thirties, but he carried himself with the confidence of someone who knew how to play the game of power.

"Mr. Costa," Elena replied, shaking his hand. "I've heard a lot about you."

"And I've heard a great deal about you as well," Costa said, gesturing for her to sit. "Your... business interests are impressive. And from what I understand, they're expanding."

Elena took a seat, her posture relaxed but her mind sharp. "Expansion always comes with risks," she said. "I'm sure you're aware of the challenges that come with growth. Especially when certain authorities take an interest in your activities."

Costa nodded, his expression serious. "That's exactly why I think we should work together. The government's crackdown on counterfeit goods is intensifying, and it's only a matter of time before they start targeting operations like yours. But with the right protection, you can continue to expand without interference."

"And what exactly are you offering, Mr. Costa?" Elena asked, her voice calm but direct.

"Power," Costa replied simply. "I'm going to be governor. And once I am, I'll have the ability to influence law enforcement, regulatory agencies, and even national policy. Your factories, your shipments—they'll be safe. I'll make sure of it."

Elena remained silent for a moment, considering his words. It was a bold offer, but one that could change everything for her. If Costa could deliver on his promises, she would have a level of protection that no other counterfeiter had ever achieved. But there was always a catch.

"And what do you want in return?" Elena asked, her eyes locked on his.

"Funding," Costa said, leaning forward slightly. "My campaign needs money—significant money. If you can provide the financial backing I need, I'll make sure your operations are never touched by law enforcement. I'll give you immunity."

Elena's mind raced as she weighed the risks and rewards. It was a dangerous game, but one she had played before. If she backed Costa and he won, she would be untouchable. But if he lost, or if he turned on her, it could all come crashing down.

After a long pause, Elena made her decision.

"I'll back you," she said finally. "But I expect results. If I don't get them, you'll regret it."

Costa smiled, his confidence unwavering. "You'll get them. I guarantee it."

# SHADOWS OF COMMERCE - THE QUEEN OF PIRACY

With Costa's campaign in full swing, Elena funneled millions of dollars into his political war chest. Her support came in the form of discreet donations, funneled through various shell companies and offshore accounts to avoid detection. In return, Costa's campaign surged ahead of his competitors, fueled by lavish events, aggressive marketing, and promises of economic reform.

As Costa's political influence grew, so did Elena's confidence in him. He was a master at playing the political game, making the right alliances, and positioning himself as the candidate of choice for both the business elite and the working class. And all the while, he never forgot the source of his financial backing.

Elena's operations benefited almost immediately from Costa's growing influence. Law enforcement agencies that had once been a threat suddenly turned a blind eye to her activities. Regulatory bodies that had scrutinized her factories and shipments now looked the other way. Her counterfeit goods continued to flow into markets across Europe, Asia, and the Middle East, unhindered by the authorities.

Costa's influence even extended beyond his own region. As his political career advanced, he formed alliances with other politicians and business leaders who could further protect Elena's interests. Her factories in remote locations, once vulnerable to raids and inspections, were now safe under the protection of corrupt officials who owed their allegiance to Costa.

Elena's empire flourished in this new environment of political protection. She was able to expand her operations even further, setting up new manufacturing plants in countries where labor was cheap, and regulations were lax. Her products, once limited to a few key markets, now reached buyers in every corner of the globe. And with Costa's help, she was able to tap into new industries and markets that had previously been out of reach.

One of the most significant benefits of Elena's alliance with Costa was her newfound ability to evade law enforcement. Before, her operations had always been at risk of raids, investigations, and seizures. But now, with Costa's protection, those risks had all but disappeared.

Costa had positioned his allies in key positions within law enforcement agencies, ensuring that any investigation into Elena's activities was either delayed or derailed entirely. Police officers, customs officials, and regulators were all on his payroll, either directly or through intermediaries. They knew that if they targeted Elena's operations, their careers—and their futures—would be at risk.

As a result, Elena's factories operated with impunity. Shipments of counterfeit goods moved freely through ports and border crossings, without fear of inspection or seizure. Her distribution networks, once vulnerable to law enforcement crackdowns, now operated smoothly and without interruption.

Even when international agencies began to take an interest in Elena's activities, Costa's influence extended beyond national borders. He had connections with politicians and officials in other countries who were willing to turn a blind eye in exchange for favors or financial incentives. Elena's empire had become a global force, and with Costa's help, she was able to navigate the complex web of international law enforcement.

As Elena's empire grew, so did her relationship with Costa. What had started as a simple business arrangement had evolved into something more—a partnership built on mutual trust, ambition, and power.

Costa's rise to political prominence had been fueled by Elena's financial support, but he had also proven himself to be a valuable ally. He had delivered on his promises, protecting Elena's operations from law enforcement and regulatory agencies. In return, Elena had continued to back him, providing the funding he needed to expand his political influence even further.

Together, they had created a powerful alliance that spanned both the business and political worlds. Elena's empire continued to expand, and Costa's political career flourished. They were unstoppable.

But as they both knew, the world of power and politics was a dangerous one. Alliances could shift, and loyalties could change. For now, they were both winning the game. But in the world they lived in, nothing was guaranteed.

Elena Marcetti had learned that lesson long ago. And while she trusted Costa—for now—she always kept her eyes open, ready for whatever might come next.

# Chapter 7: Shadows and Mirrors

Elena Marcetti sat at the head of a long mahogany table, her fingers tapping rhythmically on the polished wood. Around her, several of her most trusted advisors and business partners were discussing the latest trends in the luxury property market, the rise of new technologies in the pharmaceutical industry, and potential investments in clean energy. Elena's mind, sharp and always calculating, was taking it all in. She had come a long way from the early days of her counterfeit empire. Now, she was looking beyond that shadowy world. It was time to diversify.

The world of counterfeits had made her incredibly wealthy. Her ability to create high-quality fakes and flood the global market had turned her into a powerful figure. Yet, as her empire grew, so did the risks. She had political protection, thanks to her alliance with Mario Costa, but she knew that her success would eventually draw too much attention. Elena understood that true power lay in legitimacy. It was time to enter a new phase of her journey—one where the lines between legality and illegality blurred, where shadows and mirrors concealed the truth behind her wealth.

**It wasn't enough for Elena to be known as the queen of counterfeits. She wanted more—a legacy that couldn't be touched by the law, a fortune that would last beyond the uncertainty of the black market. She knew that to secure her future, she needed to diversify her investments, to build something real and untouchable. Her counterfeit empire would remain the bedrock of her wealth, but it would operate in the shadows, quietly funding her new ventures.**

As she sat at that table, listening to her advisors talk about the potential profits in new sectors, Elena's mind wandered to her vision of the future. She imagined herself as the head of a multinational conglomerate, a woman of power and influence in the legitimate business world. She could see herself sitting at high-profile meetings with global CEOs, attending galas and events where the elite gathered, and becoming a figure of intrigue and mystery—respected, admired, but never truly known.

Her path to legitimacy, however, had to be carefully crafted. The world she had built was one of deception, where everything was a façade. Elena knew that her transition into the legal world would require the same skill she had used to build her empire—patience, strategy, and a keen understanding of the game.

Elena's first step into the legal world was through real estate. It was a safe and time-honored way to invest money, and it provided both tangible assets and the opportunity to launder some of the immense wealth she had accumulated from her counterfeit operations. She started by buying properties in key locations across Europe, Asia, and the Middle East. Luxury apartments in major cities, beachfront villas, and commercial buildings—each acquisition was carefully chosen, not only for its profitability but also for the reputation it would help her build.

Through these acquisitions, Elena established herself as a real estate mogul, an investor with a keen eye for high-end properties. Her name began to circulate in elite circles, though no one could trace her wealth back to its true origins. Elena's team of legal experts ensured that every purchase was clean, with no visible connection to her counterfeit empire. The money was funneled through a complex network of shell companies and offshore accounts, making it impossible for authorities to trace the funds back to her illegal operations.

As her real estate portfolio grew, Elena began attending high-profile real estate conferences, luxury property exhibitions, and private investment meetings. She was no longer just a shadowy figure in the underground world of counterfeits. She was now a respected businesswoman, a player in the global real estate market.

While real estate provided Elena with a solid foundation, she knew she couldn't rely on it alone. Diversification was key, and her next move was into the world of luxury goods—this time, on the legal side. Elena had always been fascinated by fashion, and now, with her immense capital, she could enter the industry not as a counterfeiter but as a legitimate investor.

She acquired stakes in several luxury fashion brands, starting with small but prestigious boutique designers and gradually moving up to larger, well-established names. Her investments helped struggling brands expand, giving them the capital they needed to grow. In return, she gained influence in the industry, becoming a behind-the-scenes player in the world of high fashion. Her knowledge of counterfeits also gave her an edge; she knew exactly which brands were vulnerable to fakes, and she used that insight to protect her investments.

Elena's move into fashion further cemented her status in elite circles. She began attending fashion shows in Paris, Milan, and New York, always dressed impeccably in the finest couture. Designers sought her out, wanting her investment and her influence. She was becoming a public figure, but the true source of her wealth remained hidden, buried beneath layers of legitimate business deals and financial transactions.

Next, Elena expanded into the technology sector. She saw the potential in emerging industries like clean energy, biotech, and artificial intelligence. With her keen business sense, she identified startups that showed promise but lacked the funding to realize their full potential. She became a venture capitalist, funding these companies in exchange for equity. Some of her investments failed, but many succeeded, giving her a foothold in the rapidly growing tech industry.

Elena also made significant investments in pharmaceuticals, a sector she had already been involved in through her counterfeit empire. Now, however, she was operating on the legal side, funding research and development for new drugs and medical technologies. Her legitimate pharmaceutical ventures gave her access to new markets and further diversified her portfolio.

With her legal businesses flourishing, Elena's personal life began to reflect her newfound status. She purchased a private jet, ensuring she could travel the world in comfort and style. She bought a sprawling estate in the south of France, complete with a vineyard and a private beach. The estate became her retreat, a place where she could entertain high-profile guests, host lavish parties, and, most importantly, conduct business far away from prying eyes.

Elena's presence in elite social circles grew. She attended charity galas, art auctions, and exclusive events frequented by the rich and powerful. Her connections expanded beyond business and politics to include celebrities, artists, and intellectuals. Everyone was intrigued by the mysterious businesswoman who had appeared seemingly out of nowhere, with a fortune to match.

Despite the luxury and the attention, Elena never let herself forget where her wealth truly came from. The counterfeit empire she had built was still the engine that powered everything. The money she used to fund her investments, buy properties, and live a life of luxury all came from the shadows. But now, it was laundered, cleaned, and hidden behind layers of legitimacy.

Elena was careful never to flaunt her wealth too openly. She knew that in her world, too much attention could be dangerous. She maintained an air of mystery, never revealing too much about herself or her business dealings. To the public, she was a brilliant investor and businesswoman. To her closest associates, she was a force to be reckoned with—a woman who could build empires in both the shadows and the light.

Elena had always been skilled at deception. It was, after all, how she had built her counterfeit empire. But now, as she moved into the legitimate business world, the stakes were even higher. Every move she made was carefully calculated, every decision weighed for its potential risks and rewards. She had to maintain the illusion of legitimacy while keeping her illegal operations hidden.

Her team of lawyers, accountants, and advisors played a crucial role in this. They ensured that her financial transactions were untraceable, that her investments appeared clean, and that her businesses operated within the law. Elena surrounded herself with people she could trust—people who understood the game she was playing and were willing to help her navigate it.

But even with the best team, Elena knew that the danger was always present. She had enemies—rival counterfeiters, law enforcement agencies, and even some of her former partners who had turned against her. She had to stay one step ahead at all times, anticipating threats before they emerged.

In the shadows, her counterfeit empire continued to grow. New factories were being built in remote locations, and her products were flooding markets across the globe. But now, instead of simply making money, her counterfeit operations served another purpose: they funded her legal businesses. The profits from her counterfeits were funneled into her real estate ventures, her luxury brands, and her tech startups, creating a cycle of wealth that was almost impossible to trace.

As Elena's empire grew, so did the weight of the power she wielded. She had always craved control, but now that she had it, she realized that it came with a price. The more powerful she became, the more enemies she made. Rival businesspeople, politicians, and even members of the elite circles she now moved in all had their own agendas, and not all of them were friendly to Elena.

She became more paranoid, more cautious. She tightened security around her operations, hiring former military personnel to protect her factories, her shipments, and even her personal residence. She trusted fewer people, keeping her inner circle small and loyal. She knew that in her world, betrayal was always a possibility.

At the same time, she couldn't help but enjoy the fruits of her labor. The luxury, the power, the respect—it was intoxicating. Elena had spent years building her empire, and now, she was finally reaping the rewards. But she also knew that nothing lasted forever. The world she lived in was one of shadows and mirrors, where appearances could be deceiving and power could vanish in an instant.

As Elena's influence grew, so did her reputation. She became a figure of intrigue, someone people whispered about but rarely understood. Her wealth, her connections, and her mysterious past made her a topic of fascination in elite circles. Everyone wanted to know who she really was, where her money came from, and how she had risen to such heights.

But Elena remained an enigma. She gave nothing away, always maintaining an air of mystery. She was a master of deception, and she knew that in the world she inhabited, knowledge was power. The less people knew about her, the more control she had.

In the end, Elena Marcetti had built an empire that spanned both the shadows and the light. She had become a player in both the legitimate and illegitimate worlds, using one to fuel the other.

And as she looked out over the sprawling estate she had built, she knew that, for now, she had won the game.

But in the world of shadows and mirrors, victory was always fleeting.

# Chapter 8: Whispers in the Dark

Elena Marcetti sat in her luxurious office, the skyline of a bustling city framed behind her like a painting. She had built an empire that thrived in both the shadows and the light, one that made her untouchable, or so she believed. But as she stared out at the world she had conquered, there was an unsettling sense creeping in—an unease she couldn't quite place. It was as if the air had shifted, and something dangerous was lurking just beyond her reach. The whispers had begun.

For years, Elena had dominated the counterfeit market, outperforming every rival who dared challenge her. Her products were flawless replicas, indistinguishable from the real thing, and her distribution networks spanned continents. She was unrivaled, and her wealth only grew as her counterfeits flooded markets around the world. But success came with a cost—jealousy.

There were always others trying to climb the same ladder, and one of them was Klaus Reinhardt, a notorious figure in the counterfeit electronics world. He had been in the game long before Elena, but she had outsmarted and outmaneuvered him at every turn. Klaus, once a giant in the business, had seen his market share dwindle as Elena's influence spread. His factories were producing less, his buyers were turning to Elena, and his profits were shrinking.

Klaus had always been a man of pride, and watching Elena rise while he stumbled gnawed at him. He had tried competing fairly—offering cheaper prices, quicker delivery times—but none of it mattered. Elena's products were simply better, and her global network more sophisticated. Klaus knew he couldn't beat her in the marketplace. But there were other ways to win the game.

It started with a meeting. Klaus, seated across from an officer in a dimly lit café, made his move. He knew that going to the authorities was risky, but his hatred for Elena had clouded his judgment. He provided them with just enough information to pique their interest—details about certain shipments, factory locations, and key individuals involved in her operations. Klaus didn't reveal everything, of course. He wanted Elena to suffer but not at the cost of his own business.

The authorities had been watching Elena for some time, but she had always managed to stay one step ahead. Her connections in government and her army of lawyers ensured that any investigations fizzled out before they could gain traction. But Klaus's information was different. It was precise, specific, and actionable. Suddenly, the authorities had a roadmap to follow, and they began to quietly gather evidence.

At the same time, whispers of Elena's true business began circulating in the circles of power. Her rise had been meteoric, and while many admired her success, there were always those who questioned how she had amassed such a fortune so quickly. In the world of luxury real estate, fashion, and technology, reputations were everything, and Elena's was beginning to show cracks.

Rumors started to spread among business elites and political figures. Some claimed to know about her ties to the counterfeit industry, others speculated that her wealth came from far darker sources. These whispers reached the ears of people who mattered—investors, politicians, and law enforcement officials. While no one had solid proof, the mere suspicion was enough to make some of her allies uncomfortable.

One evening, at an exclusive gala in Paris, Elena overheard a conversation between two investors. They were discussing her—more specifically, her wealth. "It's odd, don't you think? How quickly she's risen? No one knows where she came from," one of them said. "I've heard things," the other replied in a hushed tone. "Things about her business. There are whispers, you know, about counterfeits."

Elena's grip on her champagne glass tightened. She kept her expression neutral, but inside, she could feel the walls beginning to close in. The rumors were spreading, and once they started, they were almost impossible to stop.

Elena knew that she had to act fast. The whispers were still just that—whispers—but if they grew louder, they could ruin everything she had built. Her first step was to strengthen her political alliances. She arranged private meetings with key politicians, offering them even more substantial financial backing in exchange for their continued support. She made it clear, without ever saying it directly, that it was in their best interest to ensure any investigations into her business went nowhere.

At the same time, Elena's legal team went into overdrive. They began reviewing all her operations, making sure that every legal front was airtight. Her legitimate businesses needed to be flawless, beyond reproach, so that if any investigation into her counterfeit empire gained traction, there would be no easy link to her legal enterprises. Shell companies were reorganized, financial records were scrubbed, and new layers of protection were put in place.

Elena also increased security at her counterfeit factories. Klaus's betrayal had made her paranoid. She had always known that competitors could turn on her, but now that it was happening, she couldn't afford to take any chances. Surveillance was tightened, employees were vetted more thoroughly, and any suspicious behavior was dealt with swiftly. Elena was determined to keep her operations running smoothly, but the stress was beginning to weigh on her.

The pressure was mounting, and with it came paranoia. Elena had always been careful about who she let into her inner circle, but now even those closest to her were under scrutiny. She began to question the loyalty of her most trusted advisors and partners. Were they loyal to her, or could they be swayed by her competitors? Were they feeding information to the authorities, or worse, to Klaus?

One evening, Elena sat in her office, staring at the profiles of her top executives. She had always been able to read people, to know when someone was lying or hiding something. But now, everyone seemed like a potential threat. She knew that Klaus's betrayal had shaken her, but she couldn't help but wonder if there were others waiting to strike.

Her chief financial officer, Marco, had been with her since the early days. He was loyal, or so she thought. But recently, he had been distant, taking more business trips than usual, and avoiding her calls. Elena had asked him about it, and he assured her that everything was fine, but she wasn't convinced. Then there was Sofia, her legal advisor. Sofia was brilliant, ruthless, and fiercely protective of Elena's interests, but she had been acting strangely as well. Could they be plotting against her?

Elena decided to take no chances. She had her security team monitor the communications of her closest associates, looking for any signs of disloyalty. She hated the idea of spying on them, but she knew that in her world, trust was a luxury she could no longer afford.

As the whispers continued to grow, Elena's world began to feel increasingly fragile. She had built her empire on deception, and now that very deception was threatening to bring it all down. The authorities had started investigating her more seriously, but they were cautious. They knew she was powerful, with deep connections in government and business. However, they also knew that if they could gather enough evidence, they could bring her down.

The first real blow came when one of Elena's smaller counterfeit factories was raided. It was a remote facility, far from her main operations, but it was still a significant loss. The authorities found enough evidence to connect the factory to her broader network, and while they hadn't yet linked it directly to Elena, it was only a matter of time before they did.

Elena's immediate response was to shut down several other smaller operations, moving production to even more remote locations and cutting ties with anyone who might be compromised. She knew that the authorities were closing in, and she couldn't afford any more slip-ups. But each step she took to protect herself only increased the tension within her organization. Employees were nervous, unsure of who they could trust, and rumors of impending raids spread like wildfire.

As Elena tightened her grip on her empire, the paranoia that had been gnawing at her began to take its toll. She became more isolated, retreating from the public eye and distancing herself from even her closest allies. Her once-impeccable public image started to crack. Invitations to elite social events became fewer, and some of her business partners began to quietly withdraw their support.

Mario Costa, the powerful politician who had once been her greatest ally, was the first to express concern. Over dinner one night, he told her in no uncertain terms that the rumors were becoming a problem. "People are talking, Elena," he said, his voice low and serious. "And not just in whispers anymore. If you don't get this under control, it could all come crashing down."

Elena listened, her face impassive, but inside she felt a rising panic. Mario was right. The whispers were no longer just in the dark corners of the business world—they were spreading. She had always believed that her wealth and power would protect her, but now she wasn't so sure. The walls were closing in, and for the first time in years, Elena felt vulnerable.

Elena knew that she was playing a dangerous game. The authorities were circling, her competitors were plotting, and the whispers about her true business were growing louder. She had built an empire that thrived in the shadows, but now those shadows were threatening to consume her.

As she sat alone in her office late one night, staring out at the city that had once seemed like hers for the taking, Elena realized that she was at a crossroads. She could continue to fight, to tighten her grip on her empire and try to silence the whispers. Or she could cut her losses, retreat into her legitimate businesses, and disappear from the world of counterfeits before it was too late.

But Elena Marcetti was not one to back down. She had fought too hard and come too far to let it all slip away. The whispers in the dark might be growing louder, but Elena was determined to silence them once and for all. She would not go down without a fight.

And so, as the world around her began to unravel, Elena prepared for the next chapter of her life. It would be dangerous, it would be treacherous, but it would also be the greatest challenge she had ever faced.

And Elena Marcetti never lost. Not in the shadows. Not in the light.

# Chapter 9: Web of Intrigue

Elena Marcetti had always been a master strategist, operating in the shadows while weaving her empire through a complex network of counterfeit production, political alliances, and legal enterprises. But now, the shadows that once protected her had become a web of intrigue, entangling her in their suffocating grip. The paranoia that had begun as a whisper in her mind was now an ever-present roar, driving her to make decisions she never thought she would have to make. The walls were closing in, and she could feel it. The authorities were circling, her political allies were becoming distant, and her carefully constructed world was starting to crumble.

The fear gnawed at her, and Elena knew that if she didn't act soon, everything she had built would come crashing down.

**It started with a subtle shift in the way people looked at her. Elena had always been a figure of intrigue, admired for her meteoric rise to success and her luxurious lifestyle. But now, those same eyes that once admired her were filled with suspicion. The rumors had grown louder, and the authorities were no longer simply watching from the sidelines—they were actively investigating.**

Several of her factories had already been raided, and though they were smaller operations designed to be disposable, the fact that the authorities had even gotten that close was enough to send a chill down Elena's spine. Each raid was a reminder that they were getting closer, and with each passing day, the noose tightened.

At first, the authorities' inquiries were quiet, almost imperceptible. A few questions here, a few records requested there. But soon, the questions became more pointed, and the people in her network began to talk. Some were being approached by investigators, and Elena knew it was only a matter of time before one of them cracked under the pressure. The whispers of her illegal dealings were now echoed in government offices and law enforcement circles, and Elena knew that the clock was ticking.

The first sign of real trouble came from one of her closest political allies, Mario Costa. For years, Mario had been one of Elena's most reliable supporters, ensuring that her business remained untouchable. In exchange for her generous financial contributions, he had kept the authorities at bay and smoothed over any regulatory issues that arose. But now, Mario was growing increasingly nervous.

During a private meeting in his office, Elena could sense the change in his demeanor. His usual confidence had been replaced by unease, and his words were careful, as if he were weighing each one before speaking.

"Elena," he said, his voice low, "there's pressure coming from higher up. People are asking questions, and I can only do so much. You need to be careful. Very careful."

Elena remained calm on the surface, but inside, a storm was brewing. She had known that the whispers were growing, but hearing it from Mario—a man who had always been in her corner—made it real. She couldn't afford to lose him, not now, not when the stakes were higher than ever.

"What are they asking?" she inquired, her tone measured.

"They're asking about your businesses, the connections between them, and the people involved. They're looking for something, Elena, and I don't know how long I can keep them off your trail."

Elena leaned back in her chair, her mind racing. She knew that she needed to tighten control, to make sure that her empire remained secure. But how? The authorities were closing in, and if her political allies started to waver, she would be left exposed.

Elena had always known how to play the game. She had built her empire not just on counterfeits but on knowing how to manipulate the system. Bribing officials was nothing new to her—it had been a crucial part of her business model from the start. But now, as the stakes grew higher, the bribes became larger, and the risks greater.

She began to funnel more money into political campaigns, targeting key figures in law enforcement and regulatory agencies. Elena knew that if she could keep these people in her pocket, she could delay or derail any investigation. It wasn't just about paying them off; it was about making sure that they were loyal to her, that they saw her success as their own.

Her meetings with these officials became more frequent, and the conversations more urgent. She promised them wealth beyond their wildest dreams, security for their families, and a share in the luxury lifestyle she enjoyed. For many, the allure was too strong to resist, and they gladly accepted her offers. But Elena knew that this was a delicate dance—one misstep, and they could turn against her just as easily as they had been bought.

As the pressure mounted, Elena turned her attention inward, scrutinizing her own people with a growing sense of mistrust. She had always prided herself on her ability to read people, to know who she could trust and who was expendable. But now, even those closest to her seemed like potential threats.

Marco, her chief financial officer, had always been loyal, but his recent behavior had raised suspicions. He had been taking more frequent trips overseas, and Elena couldn't shake the feeling that he might be hiding something. Then there was Sofia, her legal advisor, who had always been her fiercest protector. But even Sofia had been acting strangely, avoiding certain topics and appearing more guarded than usual.

Elena decided it was time to take action. She ordered her security team to begin monitoring the communications of her top executives. Every phone call, every email, every message was scrutinized for any sign of betrayal. Elena knew that if anyone within her inner circle was feeding information to the authorities or her competitors, she needed to find out before it was too late.

It wasn't long before her suspicions began to bear fruit. A conversation between Marco and an unknown contact revealed that he had been in talks with one of her rivals—Klaus Reinhardt. Elena's blood ran cold. Marco had been with her from the beginning, and yet here he was, conspiring with the man who had been trying to bring her down.

Elena had always been ruthless when necessary, but now, for the first time, she was considering measures that went beyond anything she had done before. The idea of eliminating potential threats within her own ranks had always seemed extreme, but now it didn't seem so far-fetched.

Marco was the first to be dealt with. Elena arranged for him to be "sent on a special assignment" overseas, where he would be monitored closely. She didn't have him killed—not yet—but he was no longer in a position to betray her. Sofia, on the other hand, was more difficult to handle. She was too high-profile, too deeply embedded in the legal aspects of Elena's empire to be easily removed. Elena decided to keep her close, watching her every move, waiting for the right moment to strike if necessary.

But even as Elena took these steps, the paranoia continued to eat away at her. She knew that eliminating a few potential threats wouldn't be enough. The real danger was coming from the authorities, and if her political allies turned against her, no amount of internal control would save her.

Elena's meetings with politicians became more tense. She knew they were feeling the heat, and she could sense their hesitation. They still accepted her money, but the loyalty that had once been implicit was now more fragile. Some of them had started to distance themselves, offering polite excuses for why they couldn't attend her events or why they couldn't meet as often as before.

Mario Costa, her most powerful ally, was becoming more elusive. He still took her calls, but there was a nervousness in his voice that hadn't been there before. Elena knew that he was feeling the pressure from his colleagues and from the growing investigations. She needed to ensure that he remained loyal, no matter what.

One evening, Elena invited Mario to a private dinner at her villa. Over the course of the evening, she laid out her plans for the future, emphasizing how much he stood to gain if he continued to support her. She promised him more money, more influence, and a greater share in her legitimate businesses. But she also made it clear—without ever saying it directly—that if he turned against her, there would be consequences.

Mario listened, his face impassive. When the dinner ended, he assured Elena that he would continue to have her back, but Elena wasn't convinced. The doubt in his eyes was clear. She knew that Mario was weighing his options, and that if the authorities applied enough pressure, he could easily turn on her to save himself.

Elena's empire was built on control—control over her businesses, control over her people, and control over the system that allowed her to operate. But now, that control was slipping through her fingers, and with it came a growing sense of desperation.

She began to take more drastic measures. Factories were shut down or moved to even more remote locations, employees were replaced or "let go," and security around her operations was tightened to an almost suffocating degree. But no matter what she did, Elena couldn't shake the feeling that it wasn't enough. The authorities were coming for her, and the people she had once trusted were no longer reliable.

Her days were consumed by meetings with lawyers, politicians, and security experts, all working to fortify her empire against the growing threat. But at night, when she was alone in her sprawling mansion, the paranoia would take over. She would lie awake, thinking about all the people who could betray her—the officials she had bribed, the executives who ran her businesses, the politicians who had once been her allies. Any one of them could be the weak link that brought her down.

As the days went on, Elena realized that she was playing a dangerous game. The web of intrigue she had woven was tightening around her, and she was running out of time. She had always been able to outsmart her enemies, but now, with the authorities closing in and her political allies wavering, Elena knew that her greatest challenge was yet to come.

The question was no longer whether she could keep her empire intact, but how far she was willing to go to do it. Would she be able to silence the whispers and tighten her grip on power? Or would the web of intrigue finally ensnare her, dragging her down into the shadows from which she had emerged?

Elena Marcetti had always thrived in the shadows, but now, the darkness was closing in. And this time, it wasn't clear if she would be able to escape.

# Chapter 10: New Territories, New Enemies

Elena Marcetti had always been a visionary, someone who could see beyond the limits of what most people considered possible. She had taken a small counterfeit operation and turned it into a global empire that spanned multiple industries. But with success came the inevitable hunger for more. More markets to conquer, more wealth to amass, and more power to wield. As her grip on her traditional markets strengthened, Elena's gaze turned outward to new territories—places where she had yet to establish her influence.

But in her pursuit of growth, Elena would soon discover that these new territories brought with them new enemies, each one more dangerous and unpredictable than the last. The game was changing, and the stakes were higher than ever.

**Elena's boardroom was filled with the soft glow of a world map, illuminated by the projector she had installed for just this occasion. She stood at the head of the table, her sharp gaze scanning the faces of her top executives as she outlined her new expansion strategy.**

"Latin America, Southeast Asia, Eastern Europe," Elena began, her voice calm yet commanding. "These are the regions where we will be moving next. They offer new opportunities for growth—markets with high demand, weak regulations, and, most importantly, less competition."

Her executives nodded in agreement, but there was a tension in the room that was palpable. These new territories were not as secure as the ones Elena had previously dominated. In her established markets, she had political protection, trusted allies, and a network of officials who were more than willing to turn a blind eye in exchange for bribes. But in these new regions, her influence was far less certain.

"Are you confident that we'll be able to establish the same level of control in these places?" Marco, her chief strategist, asked cautiously.

Elena smiled, though there was a sharpness to it. "It will take time. But with the right approach, the right connections, we'll succeed. We always do."

But even as she said the words, Elena knew that the road ahead would be fraught with danger. The competitors she would face in these new territories were not like the ones she had previously encountered. They were ruthless, unpredictable, and often operated in a way that left little room for negotiation. In these regions, violence was as common a tool as bribery.

Still, Elena had never been one to shy away from a challenge. She thrived on risk, and the thought of conquering these new markets excited her. The game was about to become even more dangerous, but Elena was ready to play.

Latin America was the first territory Elena set her sights on. The region had long been known for its thriving counterfeit market, with pirated goods ranging from designer clothes to pharmaceuticals flooding the streets. But it was also a region where cartel influence ran deep, and the lines between legal and illegal operations were often blurred.

Elena's team began by targeting Brazil, one of the largest and most profitable markets in the region. Her products—high-quality counterfeit luxury goods—were quickly distributed through a network of local dealers, and within months, her operations in the country were running smoothly. The demand for her goods was enormous, and the profits were even larger than she had anticipated.

But it didn't take long for Elena to attract the attention of the local players—groups who had long controlled the counterfeit market in the region. One of these was the Marquez cartel, a powerful and ruthless organization that had its hands in everything from drug trafficking to counterfeit electronics. They didn't take kindly to outsiders muscling in on their territory, and Elena's swift success had made her a target.

The first sign of trouble came in the form of a message, delivered to one of Elena's distributors in Rio de Janeiro. It was a simple note, written in Portuguese, but its meaning was clear:
"Get out, or you won't live to see another sunrise."

The distributor, terrified, brought the message directly to Elena's attention. She dismissed it at first, chalking it up to idle threats from a competitor who was feeling the pressure of her success. But as more messages followed, each one more menacing than the last, Elena knew she had to take the threat seriously.

She called a meeting with her security team, who advised her to halt operations in Brazil temporarily until they could assess the situation further. But Elena refused. Halting operations would be seen as a sign of weakness, and she had never backed down from a challenge.

Instead, she decided to take matters into her own hands. She reached out to one of her political contacts in the region—a local senator with ties to the police force. For a hefty price, he agreed to provide protection for her operations, ensuring that the Marquez cartel would think twice before making any move against her.

For a time, it seemed to work. Her products continued to flood the market, and the threats subsided. But Elena knew that the peace was fragile. The Marquez cartel wasn't the type to be easily intimidated, and she had a feeling that they were simply biding their time, waiting for the right moment to strike.

As her operations in Latin America continued, Elena shifted her attention to Southeast Asia—a region with booming economies and a growing demand for luxury goods. The markets in Thailand, Indonesia, and Vietnam were ripe for the taking, and Elena wasted no time in establishing a presence there.

But Southeast Asia presented a different set of challenges. Unlike Latin America, where the threat came primarily from rival criminal organizations, Southeast Asia's counterfeit market was deeply entrenched in local cultures and economies. In many of these countries, counterfeiting was seen not just as a business but as a way of life, with entire communities dependent on the production and sale of fake goods.

Elena's entry into these markets was met with suspicion and resistance from local counterfeit producers, who saw her as a foreign invader threatening their livelihood. In Indonesia, a group of local counterfeiters banded together to form an alliance, vowing to keep Elena's products out of the country.

But Elena was undeterred. She knew that money spoke louder than loyalty, and she began to systematically buy out the leaders of these local counterfeiting networks, offering them more money than they could ever dream of. One by one, they fell in line, and soon, Elena's products were being sold alongside their own.

However, the deeper she expanded into Southeast Asia, the more dangerous the situation became. In Thailand, Elena ran into trouble with a group of counterfeit electronics producers who had ties to the military. They were well-connected and had no qualms about using violence to protect their turf. Elena's team was forced to pay exorbitant bribes to local officials just to keep their operations running, and even then, the threat of violence hung in the air.

Eastern Europe was perhaps the most dangerous territory Elena had ever entered. The region was known for its thriving black market, and the competition was fierce. Unlike in Latin America or Southeast Asia, where she could rely on political protection and bribery to keep her operations safe, Eastern Europe was a different story.

Here, the counterfeit market was controlled by powerful criminal syndicates with ties to the Russian mafia. These were men who played by a different set of rules—men who didn't hesitate to use violence, intimidation, and even assassination to protect their interests.

Elena knew that expanding into Eastern Europe would be risky, but the potential profits were too great to ignore. Her team began by targeting Hungary, Romania, and Poland—countries with growing economies and a high demand for luxury goods. But it didn't take long for her to realize that she was stepping into a hornet's nest.

In Romania, one of her warehouses was firebombed by a local gang that had been paid off by one of her competitors. In Hungary, several of her distributors were kidnapped and held for ransom, forcing Elena to pay millions just to get them back alive. And in Poland, the authorities—many of whom were in the pockets of the local mafia—began to crack down on her operations, making it nearly impossible to move her products.

Elena was no stranger to danger, but even she couldn't deny that Eastern Europe was a different beast. The competition was ruthless, and the consequences of failure were deadly.

As Elena expanded into these new territories, the cost of doing business continued to rise. The bribes she had to pay to local officials were higher than ever, and the risk of violence loomed large. Her security costs skyrocketed as she was forced to hire private militias and bodyguards to protect her warehouses, distributors, and even herself.

But despite the growing dangers, Elena pressed on. She had always thrived on risk, and the challenges she faced only fueled her desire to succeed. She knew that if she could conquer these new territories, her empire would be stronger than ever.

But there was a growing sense of unease in the air. Elena's enemies were becoming more dangerous, and the threats more personal. She had always been able to outmaneuver her competitors, but now, she was up against forces that were beyond her control.

In the face of these new threats, Elena began to forge new alliances. In Latin America, she reached out to rival cartels, offering them a share of her profits in exchange for protection. In Southeast Asia, she began to work more closely with local government officials, ensuring that they had a vested interest in keeping her operations safe. And in Eastern Europe, she sought out powerful allies within the criminal underworld, offering them a cut of her business in exchange for their support.

These new alliances came at a cost, but they were necessary for survival. Elena knew that in these new territories, she couldn't rely solely on her own strength. She needed allies—people who could protect her from the enemies that were closing in from all sides.

But even as she forged these new alliances, Elena couldn't shake the feeling that the walls were closing in. The risks were greater than ever, and the enemies she was making were more dangerous than any she had faced before.

As Elena continued to expand into new territories, she knew that she was taking a dangerous gamble. The competitors she faced in these regions were ruthless, and the consequences of failure were more severe than ever. But Elena had always thrived on risk, and she wasn't about to back down now.

The question was no longer whether she could succeed, but how far she was willing to go to protect her empire. Would she be able to outmaneuver her new enemies, or would they finally bring her down?

Elena Marcetti had built her empire on a foundation of risk and ambition, but now, as she ventured into new territories, she was playing a game that was more dangerous than ever. And this time, the stakes were higher than she could have ever imagined.

# Chapter 11: A Powerful Ally Lost

Elena Marcetti stood at the peak of her empire, but with every empire comes the risk of collapse. Over the years, she had carefully crafted an intricate web of power, influence, and alliances, with political allies being some of her most critical assets. Among these, none was more crucial than her relationship with Senator Alessandro De Luca. He had been her most trusted political ally for years, his influence shielding her from the authorities and allowing her operations to thrive. But now, that relationship was crumbling, and with it, the protective shield Elena had relied on for so long.

A single misunderstanding, a slight misstep in a business deal, had turned Senator De Luca from a powerful friend to a dangerous enemy. And without his protection, Elena's empire was beginning to feel the weight of exposure to both legal threats and criminal rivals.

**It had started with what seemed like a routine business transaction. Senator De Luca had grown accustomed to Elena's generosity, particularly when it came to funding his political campaigns and ensuring his lavish lifestyle. In return, he had been her shield, keeping the authorities at bay and smoothing over any legal hiccups that came her way. It was an arrangement that had worked flawlessly for years—until it didn't.**

The misunderstanding came when Elena had begun her expansion into Southeast Asia. De Luca had suggested a particular business deal involving government contracts for infrastructure projects in exchange for continued political support. It was a high-stakes venture that required careful maneuvering, with significant bribes and connections being thrown into play.

However, Elena had her eyes set elsewhere. With the expansion of her counterfeit empire into new and dangerous territories, she needed to prioritize protecting her core operations and finding new revenue streams. She had made the decision to withdraw from the infrastructure deal at the last moment, redirecting funds toward bolstering her security in Southeast Asia and Eastern Europe. It was a calculated move, one she believed would protect her empire from more immediate threats.

But De Luca saw it as a betrayal.

He had invested significant political capital in ensuring the deal's success, and Elena's withdrawal left him exposed. The senator had counted on those contracts to fund his next re-election campaign, and without them, he faced serious political backlash. What was worse, it wasn't just the financial aspect that wounded him—it was the perception that Elena had put her own interests above their longstanding alliance.

At first, the rift between Elena and De Luca was subtle. He stopped returning her calls as promptly as he used to, and when they did meet, the warmth that once characterized their conversations was replaced by cold, calculated exchanges. Elena, astute as ever, picked up on the shift immediately, but she was confident that the situation could be salvaged. After all, she had weathered worse storms before.

She arranged a private dinner at an exclusive restaurant in Rome, hoping to smooth things over. As she sat across from De Luca, she could sense the tension in his posture, the barely concealed anger simmering beneath his calm façade.

"Elena," he began, his voice cool, "I think we need to have a serious conversation about where our priorities lie."

Elena smiled, attempting to disarm him with her charm. "Alessandro, you know I value our relationship above all else. The deal—"

"The deal was everything," De Luca interrupted, his tone sharper than she'd ever heard it before. "You backed out when I needed you most, Elena. You left me exposed. Do you understand what kind of position that puts me in?"

"I had to make a decision," she explained, keeping her voice steady. "I needed to protect our long-term interests. There were new threats, new competitors. The infrastructure deal wasn't going to provide the security we needed."

De Luca shook his head, leaning back in his chair. "You think too short-term, Elena. This wasn't just about money—it was about influence, power. You've built an empire, but empires fall if they don't have the right people in their corner."

For the first time in years, Elena felt a wave of uncertainty wash over her. She had always been in control, always one step ahead. But now, she was facing the possibility of losing her most powerful ally, and she wasn't sure how to stop it.

"I'll make it right," she promised. "Tell me what you need."

De Luca's gaze hardened. "It's too late for that."

With De Luca's backing gone, Elena's empire was suddenly vulnerable. For years, she had operated in the shadows, her counterfeit empire flourishing under the radar thanks to the senator's protection. He had ensured that the authorities stayed away from her operations, and his influence had smoothed over any legal obstacles that arose. But now, that protection was gone.

It didn't take long for the cracks to appear. Local authorities in several countries began launching investigations into her businesses, inquiries that had previously been stalled by De Luca's intervention. Police raids on her warehouses in Italy, Spain, and

Southeast Asia disrupted her supply chains, costing her millions in lost products. Several of her key distributors were arrested, and while Elena was able to bail some of them out, the damage was already done. Her once tight-knit network of loyal distributors was starting to fray as fear spread through the ranks.

But the legal threats were only half of the problem. Without De Luca's protection, Elena's rivals saw an opportunity to move in on her territory. The Marquez cartel in Latin America began pushing harder, using intimidation tactics and violence to take over her distribution channels. In Eastern Europe, her competitors in the counterfeit electronics market became bolder, encroaching on her territory without fear of political repercussions.

Elena's empire, once a well-oiled machine, was now teetering on the edge of chaos.

Elena was no stranger to adversity. She had built her empire from the ground up, navigating treacherous waters and outsmarting rivals at every turn. But this time was different. This time, the stakes were higher, and the enemies more dangerous. She knew that without political protection, her empire wouldn't survive for long.

Desperate to find a new ally, Elena began reaching out to other politicians, business leaders, and influential figures, hoping to secure the support she needed to maintain her grip on power. She hosted lavish parties, offered generous donations, and made promises of lucrative business deals. But none of it seemed to be enough.

De Luca's influence had been far-reaching, and without his backing, many of the people Elena approached were hesitant to get involved. They knew the risks that came with aligning themselves with her, especially now that her business was under increased scrutiny from the authorities.

Frustration began to set in. Elena had always prided herself on her ability to manipulate and charm those around her, but now, her usual tactics were failing. She was running out of options, and time was running out.

As the pressure mounted, tensions within Elena's organization began to rise. Her lieutenants, once fiercely loyal, started questioning her decisions. Some believed that she had grown too ambitious, expanding too quickly into new territories without securing the necessary protections. Others whispered that her judgment had been clouded by greed, that she had overplayed her hand with De Luca and was now paying the price.

Marco, her chief strategist, was one of the few who remained steadfast in his loyalty, but even he couldn't hide his concerns. During a tense meeting with Elena, he voiced what others had been too afraid to say.

"Elena, we're exposed," Marco said, his voice low but firm. "Without De Luca, we're vulnerable to both the authorities and our competitors. We need to pull back, regroup, and find a way to stabilize the situation before it gets worse."

Elena's eyes narrowed. "You think I don't know that? I'm working on it, Marco. We'll find a way through this."

"I'm not doubting your abilities," Marco replied carefully. "But we can't afford any more missteps. If we don't act soon, this whole thing could come crashing down."

Elena knew he was right, but the thought of pulling back, of retreating from the empire she had spent years building, was unbearable. She had always been a fighter, always found a way to come out on top. But now, for the first time, she felt the weight of doubt pressing down on her.

As Elena scrambled to regain control, her rivals continued to close in. The Marquez cartel ramped up their efforts in Latin America, taking over several of her key distribution routes and cutting off her supply chains. In Eastern Europe, her competitors had formed an alliance, pooling their resources to outmaneuver her in the counterfeit electronics market.

But the most dangerous threat came from within her own ranks. Several of her top lieutenants, sensing weakness, began making moves behind her back, forming alliances with her rivals and plotting to take over her operations. Betrayal was a constant risk in the world Elena operated in, but now, it seemed closer than ever.

One of her most trusted lieutenants, Franco, had been secretly meeting with a rival cartel in Mexico, negotiating a deal to sell them access to Elena's distribution network in exchange for protection. When Elena found out, she was furious. She confronted Franco in her office, her anger barely contained.

"You think you can betray me and get away with it?" Elena hissed, her eyes blazing with fury.

Franco didn't flinch. "You're losing control, Elena. The Marquez cartel is taking over Latin America, the Russians are pushing us out of Eastern Europe, and the authorities are breathing down our necks. If we don't make a move now, we're all going to lose."

Elena's hand trembled with rage as she grabbed a letter opener from her desk, her mind racing with thoughts of revenge. But she stopped herself. Killing Franco wouldn't solve her problems. If anything, it would only make things worse.

Instead, she took a deep breath and forced herself to think strategically. Franco was right—she was losing control. But she wasn't ready to give up just yet.

As the days turned into weeks, Elena's situation continued to deteriorate. Without De Luca's protection, the authorities were closing in faster than she could manage. Her enemies, both within and outside her organization, were growing bolder, sensing that her time at the top was coming to an end.

Elena had always thrived on risk, but now, the odds were stacked against her. She was running out of time, out of allies, and out of options.

And for the first time in her life, she felt the chilling grip of fear tightening around her heart.

# Chapter 12: Cracks in the Empire

The opulent life Elena Marcetti had worked so hard to build now felt like a fragile illusion, ready to shatter at the slightest touch. The air of invincibility that had once surrounded her was crumbling, and for the first time in years, she found herself facing an uncertain future. Her empire, which had always operated like a well-oiled machine, was now riddled with cracks, and the rumors of her illegal dealings were beginning to spiral out of control.

The press had caught wind of whispers about her counterfeit operation, and while no solid evidence had been brought to the surface yet, the rumors alone were enough to attract the attention of government agencies. Elena had been in the game long enough to know that when the press started sniffing around, it was only a matter of time before the authorities followed. Worse still, the rumors weren't just the result of speculation—they were being fed by people within her own ranks.

Some of her most trusted allies, sensing that her empire was in decline, were turning on her to protect their own interests. Loyalty, in this world, was a luxury no one could afford for long, and the cracks in her empire were widening faster than Elena could repair them.

**It had started with a few murmurs in elite circles—small, seemingly innocuous conversations at high-society galas or exclusive business dinners. Whispers about how Elena's wealth had grown suspiciously fast, how her rise to prominence didn't quite add up. These whispers might have been easy to dismiss, but they had a way of snowballing.**

**Within weeks, rumors about Elena's business dealings began to circulate in the media. Gossip columns and financial papers hinted**

at connections between her luxury brand empire and illegal counterfeit operations, though no one dared to print the full story. But that was enough to get the attention of the government.

One morning, as Elena sat in her study overlooking the sprawling gardens of her Roman estate, she received a phone call from her PR advisor, Sofia. There was an edge of panic in her voice that Elena had never heard before.

"Elena, we've got a problem," Sofia said, her words clipped. "There's a reporter from *Il Messaggero* who's been digging into your background for weeks. I think they're about to publish something, and it's not going to be pretty."

Elena felt her stomach clench, but she kept her voice steady. "What exactly are they planning to write?"

Sofia hesitated before answering. "They've been speaking to some of your former business associates—people who were involved in your expansion in Eastern Europe. They're claiming that a significant part of your empire was built on counterfeit goods. It's still rumors at this point, but they're saying they have sources willing to go on record."

Elena leaned back in her chair, her mind racing. She had always been careful, always ensured that her illegal dealings were buried beneath layers of legitimate business fronts. But she had also known that it was only a matter of time before someone tried to expose her.

"Who are these sources?" Elena asked, her voice cold.

"I don't know," Sofia admitted. "But if the press starts publishing these stories, the authorities are going to take notice. We need to contain this."

Elena nodded, though she already knew what had to be done. The press could be managed, silenced with enough money and threats. But the real danger wasn't the reporters—it was the people within her own circle who were leaking information. If her closest allies were turning against her, she needed to act fast.

Elena's empire had been built on trust, or at least the appearance of it. She had surrounded herself with loyalists, people who had benefitted from her success and, in turn, protected her interests. But now, as the rumors began to spread, the loyalty she had once relied on was eroding.

One of the first betrayals came from an unexpected place—Giovanni Russo, her legal advisor and one of her oldest associates. Giovanni had been by her side for years, navigating the legal gray areas that allowed her counterfeit operation to flourish without attracting too much attention. He had always been discreet, fiercely loyal to Elena's cause. Or so she had thought.

Late one evening, Elena received an anonymous tip that Giovanni had been meeting with investigators from the Italian Financial Police. It seemed impossible at first—Giovanni had always been the one to cover her tracks, to ensure that no one could connect her legitimate businesses with the counterfeit empire she ran in the shadows. But as Elena dug deeper, the truth became undeniable.

Giovanni, it turned out, had struck a deal. Facing pressure from investigators who had uncovered irregularities in his own dealings, he had decided to save himself by feeding them information about Elena's operation. He had betrayed her to protect his own interests, just as so many others were beginning to do.

When Elena confronted him, it was in a quiet corner of her private office, far away from prying eyes. Giovanni sat across from her, his face pale, his hands trembling slightly.

"You know why you're here," Elena said, her voice ice cold.

Giovanni nodded, though he couldn't meet her gaze. "Elena, I didn't have a choice. They were going to come after me. I had to—"

"You had to betray me," she finished for him, her eyes narrowing. "After everything I've done for you, you sold me out to save your own skin."

"Elena, please," Giovanni pleaded. "They have evidence. If I didn't cooperate, they would have put me in prison. I—"

"I don't care about your excuses," Elena snapped, cutting him off. "You were supposed to protect me. And now you've left me exposed."

For a long moment, there was silence between them. Giovanni shifted nervously in his seat, his eyes darting to the door as if he were considering making a run for it. But Elena had already made up her mind.

"I want you out of my sight," she said, her voice low and dangerous. "If I ever see you again, I won't hesitate to end you."

Giovanni didn't need to be told twice. He stood, mumbling apologies as he backed toward the door. But as he left, Elena knew that this was just the beginning. Giovanni was one crack in the foundation, but there would be others.

With Giovanni's betrayal confirmed, Elena knew that the media rumors would soon escalate. She had tried to control the narrative, to pay off reporters and use her influence to silence the press. But the story was too big to contain, and soon, the headlines were impossible to ignore.

*"The Empire Behind the Facade: Elena Marcetti's Counterfeit Fortune"* screamed one headline. *"Luxury or Lies? The Shady World of Marcetti Enterprises"* read another.

Elena's name, once synonymous with luxury and success, was now being dragged through the mud. And while the press didn't have concrete proof of her involvement in the counterfeit world, the whispers were enough to damage her reputation.

Her legitimate businesses began to suffer. Investors, once eager to partner with her, started to pull out of deals. Her properties, once highly sought after, were suddenly viewed with suspicion. Even her elite social circle began to distance themselves, fearful of being associated with the growing scandal.

For the first time in her career, Elena found herself on the defensive, trying to protect her crumbling empire from both the media and the authorities.

As the rumors continued to spread, Elena knew that her only chance of survival was to reinforce the facade of legitimacy that had protected her for so long. She intensified her efforts to cover up the truth, bribing officials and threatening those who dared to question her.

But the cracks were growing wider. Her once-loyal lieutenants, sensing that her empire was in jeopardy, began to turn on her. Some, like Giovanni, struck deals with the authorities to save themselves. Others simply disappeared, fleeing before the collapse could take them down with it.

Elena's paranoia grew by the day. She began to suspect everyone around her of betrayal, questioning the loyalty of even her closest confidants. She tightened her inner circle, cutting off anyone who she believed could pose a threat. But in doing so, she isolated herself even further.

The empire she had spent years building was slowly unraveling, and Elena was running out of allies.

In a last-ditch effort to save her empire, Elena made a bold and dangerous move. She decided to shift her focus away from Europe, where the authorities were closing in, and expand her operations into new, uncharted territories. She believed that by moving her counterfeit empire to regions where law enforcement was weaker and corruption more rampant, she could buy herself time to rebuild.

It was a risky gamble, but Elena had always thrived on risk. She sent her most trusted lieutenants to scout new markets in Africa, South America, and parts of the Middle East. The plan was to establish new distribution channels and create a fresh network of allies who could protect her interests in these regions.

But the move came with its own set of dangers. The new territories were fraught with their own political instability and dangerous criminal organizations, many of which were more ruthless than anything Elena had encountered before. She was stepping into unknown territory, and one wrong move could be fatal.

Back home, the cracks in Elena's empire were turning into full-blown fissures. The betrayal of Giovanni had been just the beginning. Several of her top lieutenants were now openly challenging her authority, questioning her leadership and making moves to take over parts of her operation.

Marco, her chief strategist, had always been ambitious, but now he saw an opportunity to seize control. Elena had noticed the shift in his behavior—he was no longer as deferential as he once was. He had begun making decisions without consulting her, forging alliances with factions within her organization that were loyal to him rather than to her.

Elena knew that if she didn't act quickly, Marco would attempt a coup. But she also knew that taking him out would send shockwaves through her already weakened organization. The infighting was tearing her empire apart, and every decision she made now had the potential to either save or destroy everything she had built.

As Elena sat in her penthouse office, overlooking the city that had once been her playground, she realized that the empire she had worked so hard to build was slipping through her fingers. The rumors, the betrayals, the media storm—it was all coming to a head, and there was little she could do to stop it.

Her once-loyal allies were turning against her, and the cracks in her empire were growing wider by the day. She was still Elena Marcetti, still one of the most powerful figures in the world of luxury and counterfeit goods. But for how much longer?

Elena's empire was crumbling, and she knew that the worst was yet to come. The cracks had become too deep, and soon, everything she had built would come crashing down.

And when it did, she would be left standing alone in the ruins of her once-great kingdom.

# Chapter 13: The Media's Eye

Elena Marcetti's empire was under siege, but this time, the attack didn't come from rival businesses or disgruntled former allies. It came from an entirely different source—the press. The media had always been a powerful force, but now, it had become Elena's worst enemy. Her once-glamorous image was being picked apart by journalists who had grown suspicious of her meteoric rise to wealth and power. And though no one knew the full truth yet, the threads were starting to unravel.

The first real blow came in the form of an investigative report by *Il Messaggero*, one of Italy's most respected newspapers. It was a detailed piece that delved into Elena's business ventures, pointing out the inconsistencies in her success story. The article raised questions about how a relatively unknown entrepreneur could have amassed such a vast fortune in such a short amount of time. The report stopped short of making direct accusations but hinted at darker undercurrents in Elena's rise to power.

**Journalists, as Elena had always known, were persistent creatures. Once they caught the scent of a story, they wouldn't let go. The article in** *Il Messaggero* **was just the beginning, the first ripple in what would soon become a tidal wave of scrutiny. Other news outlets began to pick up the story, each adding their own spin to the narrative. Speculation swirled about how Elena had built her luxury empire, and the more the media probed, the more cracks they found.**

At first, the questions seemed benign. Reports focused on her rapid success, her luxurious lifestyle, and her seemingly endless list of connections in high society. But it didn't take long for the tone to shift. Journalists began to dig deeper into her business practices, looking for any signs of foul play. They examined her company's financial records, interviewed former employees, and started connecting the dots between her legal ventures and the shadowy world of counterfeit goods.

Elena had always known that her success was built on a delicate balance of legitimate business and illegal activity. But for years, she had managed to keep the two worlds separate enough to avoid detection. Now, that separation was starting to blur in the public eye.

As the media frenzy intensified, a new nickname began to circulate in the headlines: "The Queen of Piracy." It was a title that both fascinated and horrified the public. On the surface, Elena was still seen as a glamorous, powerful businesswoman, a symbol of success. But beneath that polished exterior, the rumors painted a different picture. The Queen of Piracy was a woman who had built her empire on stolen ideas and counterfeit goods, using her charm and connections to stay one step ahead of the law.

The nickname stuck, and soon, it was everywhere. Tabloid newspapers splashed it across their front pages, while business journals used it in more measured tones. Social media lit up with speculation, with everyone from bloggers to influencers discussing whether Elena was truly the mastermind behind a global counterfeit empire.

For Elena, the nickname was a double-edged sword. On the one hand, it kept her in the public eye, reinforcing her status as one of the most powerful women in the world. But on the other, it was a constant reminder that her carefully constructed image was unraveling. The more the media dug into her past, the more vulnerable she became.

Among the many journalists investigating Elena, one stood out: Marco DeLuca, an investigative reporter who had built a reputation for uncovering corporate corruption. He had been following Elena's rise for months, long before the rumors of her illegal dealings had reached the mainstream media. Marco had a knack for finding the truth, and now, he was determined to expose the real story behind Elena Marcetti.

Marco's investigation was relentless. He interviewed former employees, digging up old grievances and unearthing stories of questionable business practices. Some of these employees had worked in her luxury brand empire, while others had been involved in her overseas operations, where the lines between legal and illegal activity were often blurred. What he found was a web of secrecy, a carefully constructed facade that masked a much darker reality.

Marco's big break came when he managed to track down one of Elena's former lieutenants—a man who had worked closely with her during her expansion into Eastern Europe. The man, who had since fled the country to avoid prosecution, was willing to talk in exchange for anonymity and protection. What he revealed confirmed much of what Marco had suspected: Elena's business empire had been built, at least in part, on counterfeit goods. Her luxury brand, which had made her famous, was funded by a sprawling network of illegal operations that produced knock-offs of high-end products.

Marco knew he had the story of a lifetime. But he also knew that publishing it would be risky. Elena had powerful connections, and she wasn't the kind of woman to take threats lightly. Still, Marco was determined to move forward. He had seen too many powerful people escape justice because of their wealth and influence. This time, he vowed, would be different.

Elena, meanwhile, was fully aware that the walls were closing in. She had managed to survive the initial wave of rumors by keeping a tight grip on her public image, but now, the situation was spiraling out of control. The nickname "Queen of Piracy" had become a permanent fixture in the media, and the investigations into her business practices were becoming more aggressive by the day.

Her PR team worked around the clock to manage the fallout. Press releases were issued denying any involvement in illegal activities, and Elena herself made a series of high-profile public appearances, always dressed impeccably, always calm and composed. She hosted charity events, gave interviews where she spoke about empowering women in business, and continued to present herself as a model of success.

But behind the scenes, Elena was scrambling. Her legal team was preparing for the worst, knowing that if the allegations gained traction, she could face serious consequences—not just for her business, but for her own freedom. And more troubling still, Elena was losing control over the people who had once been loyal to her.

Several of her former associates, sensing that the empire was on the verge of collapse, had begun to distance themselves. Some had even started cooperating with the media, feeding them information in exchange for anonymity. It was a dangerous game, and Elena knew it. The cracks in her empire were widening, and there was only so much she could do to contain the damage.

As the media investigation continued, public opinion began to shift. For years, Elena had been admired for her success, her style, and her seemingly unshakable confidence. But now, the public was beginning to question the woman behind the brand. The nickname "Queen of Piracy" had started as a rumor, but now it was becoming an identity—a symbol of corruption, deceit, and greed.

People who had once been her most loyal customers were now boycotting her brands. Social media campaigns urged consumers to avoid her products, accusing her of profiting from stolen ideas and exploiting workers in her counterfeit operations. The luxury stores that had once proudly displayed her merchandise were starting to reconsider their partnerships, fearful of being tainted by the growing scandal.

Elena had always thrived on attention, but now, the spotlight was turning against her. Every move she made was scrutinized, every statement dissected by journalists eager for the next piece of the puzzle. And while she had always been able to manipulate the media to her advantage, this time, the narrative was slipping out of her control.

The growing media attention on Elena's business practices didn't go unnoticed by the authorities. Government agencies, which had been watching Elena's empire from the shadows for years, were now feeling the pressure to take action. The rumors of her involvement in counterfeit operations had been circulating in law enforcement circles for a long time, but without concrete evidence, there had been little they could do.

Now, however, the media's investigation was providing the authorities with the leads they needed. The articles published by Marco DeLuca and others were filled with details that hinted at the existence of a vast, underground network of counterfeit production. Investigators began to quietly collect information, interviewing former employees, examining financial records, and building a case against Elena.

For Elena, this was the worst possible outcome. The media had always been a threat to her reputation, but the government posed a much greater danger. If the authorities managed to link her luxury empire to illegal activities, it wouldn't just be her image that was damaged—it would be the end of her empire altogether. She could face prison time, lose her businesses, and forfeit the fortune she had spent years amassing.

But Elena wasn't ready to give up. She had faced challenges before, and she had always found a way to survive. This time, though, the stakes were higher than ever.

As the media's investigation intensified, Elena found herself fighting on multiple fronts. She was trying to maintain control of her empire, fend off government investigations, and protect her public image—all while managing the growing sense of betrayal from within her own ranks.

She had always prided herself on her ability to stay ahead of her enemies, but now, she was struggling to keep up. The media was relentless, and every day brought new allegations, new stories, and new threats to her empire. Her legal team was working around the clock, but even they knew that they were running out of options.

Elena's fight for survival became more desperate with each passing day. She doubled down on her efforts to silence the press, offering bribes to journalists, threatening lawsuits, and using her remaining political connections to stall the government investigation. But the media wasn't backing down, and neither were the authorities.

For the first time in her life, Elena Marcetti—the Queen of Piracy—was losing control. And as the cracks in her empire widened, she realized that the real battle had only just begun.

The media's relentless pursuit of the truth had begun to take its toll on Elena's empire. What had started as a few whispers of suspicion had now grown into a full-blown investigation, with the public, the press, and the government all watching her every move.

Elena knew that the worst was still to come. The media had only scratched the surface of her empire's dark underbelly, and as the investigations continued, it was only a matter of time before the full truth was exposed.

For now, Elena remained defiant, determined to fight to keep her empire intact. But deep down, she knew that the tides were turning against her. And as she stood on the brink of losing everything, she couldn't help but wonder: how much longer could she hold on?

# Chapter 14: Scrambling for Control

The weight of everything was closing in on Elena Marcetti. The investigations, the press, the whispers of betrayal—it was all tightening around her like a noose. For years, she had carefully crafted an empire, built on a mixture of legitimate business and shadowy dealings that stayed just out of reach of the law. But now, all of it seemed to be crumbling beneath her.

Her once-stable world was fracturing, and as each day passed, the cracks in her empire widened. Elena was no longer in the comfortable position of maneuvering from the shadows. She was fighting for survival in the harsh light of public scrutiny and under the prying eyes of law enforcement. The Queen of Piracy, as the media had dubbed her, was scrambling to keep her empire intact, but it was slipping through her fingers.

**The investigations had grown more aggressive. Government agencies were no longer just quietly observing—they were gathering evidence, following leads provided by the media's reports, and subpoenaing documents. Elena's financial records were being pored over by forensic accountants, and the more they dug, the more irregularities they found. Money was being traced back to shell companies, offshore accounts, and other hidden assets that were clearly designed to obfuscate the true nature of her wealth.**

Even worse, the people around her were starting to crumble. Former allies were distancing themselves, hoping to avoid being dragged down with her. Some were even turning against her, offering information to the authorities in exchange for immunity or lighter sentences. It was as though a dam had broken, and everyone who had once been loyal to her was now jumping ship.

Elena's phone rang constantly—lawyers, business associates, political contacts, all trying to get updates on what was happening, some offering their support, while others were subtly making their exit. The fear in their voices was unmistakable. They knew that the empire was at risk of collapse, and they didn't want to be caught in the debris when it all came crashing down.

Elena, however, refused to let go of control. She had built this empire with her bare hands, clawing her way to the top, and she wasn't about to let it all slip away without a fight.

The first thing Elena did was call in favors. She had powerful contacts in government, people who owed her for past favors, and now she needed them to repay their debts. She reached out to high-ranking officials, hoping to delay the investigations or, at the very least, slow down the legal processes. Some were sympathetic, but many were wary. Elena was no longer the untouchable business mogul they had once admired—she was a liability. Helping her could damage their own careers or worse, implicate them in her schemes.

Still, Elena managed to secure a few extensions, buying herself time to reorganize her defenses. But time was running out faster than she could contain the damage. The press was relentless, and with every new article, public perception of her grew darker. The once-respected Elena Marcetti was now seen as a corrupt, manipulative figure who had built her empire on lies and deception. The headlines called her a "fraud," a "thief," and the infamous "Queen of Piracy" title followed her everywhere.

Elena's PR team worked tirelessly to counter the negative press. They issued statements denying the allegations, painting Elena as the victim of a media witch hunt. She appeared in interviews, maintaining her calm and composed demeanor, speaking about her philanthropic work and her desire to empower women in business. But the more she tried to control the narrative, the more it slipped out of her hands. Public sentiment was turning against her, and no amount of damage control could reverse the tide.

As the pressure mounted, Elena began to see betrayal everywhere. The stress of constant legal threats, the negative media attention, and the sense that her empire was collapsing all around her made her increasingly paranoid. She had built her success by trusting very few people, and now even those few seemed suspect.

Her first major act of desperation came when she discovered that one of her senior executives had been secretly meeting with government investigators. It was a betrayal Elena hadn't seen coming. This executive had been with her since the early days, someone she had trusted implicitly. But as it turned out, when faced with the threat of prosecution, the executive had chosen self-preservation over loyalty.

Elena reacted swiftly and ruthlessly. She had the executive removed from their position immediately, using her influence to ensure that they were blacklisted from the industry. But it didn't stop there. In private, Elena's paranoia took over. She became convinced that this was just the beginning, that there were more traitors in her midst—people who would turn on her the moment it became convenient.

To protect herself, she launched her own internal investigation, hiring private investigators to monitor her employees and business associates. She began listening in on phone calls, reviewing emails, and tracking her staff's movements. No one was above suspicion, not even those closest to her. Elena was no longer just trying to defend her empire—she was hunting down anyone who could potentially betray her.

The deeper Elena sank into her paranoia, the more ruthless she became. She no longer saw people as allies or employees—they were either assets or threats. Those who were loyal were rewarded, but those she suspected of disloyalty were swiftly dealt with.

One by one, people began to disappear from her inner circle. Some were forced out of the company under the guise of "downsizing" or "restructuring." Others simply vanished, their careers destroyed by whispers that Elena had planted to discredit them. The more paranoid Elena became, the more she isolated herself from the people she had once trusted.

Her ruthlessness didn't stop at the boardroom. She had built her empire by knowing how to control people, and now, she used that skill to protect herself. If someone posed a threat—whether it was a former employee, a competitor, or even a business partner—Elena didn't hesitate to eliminate them. Bribery, blackmail, intimidation—nothing was off the table. She had contacts in the criminal underworld, and she wasn't afraid to use them.

In some cases, Elena resorted to even more drastic measures. Those who posed the greatest threat to her—those who knew too much or were in positions to bring her down—simply disappeared. Elena was careful, of course, always making sure that nothing could be traced back to her. But the disappearances sent a clear message to anyone who might consider betraying her: cross Elena Marcetti, and you would pay the price.

As the rumors of her ruthlessness spread, even the media began to feel her wrath. Journalists who had been investigating her found themselves facing legal threats and intimidation. Some received anonymous warnings, telling them to back off if they valued their safety. A few of the more persistent reporters had their personal lives exposed in the tabloids, with damaging stories that seemed to come out of nowhere.

Elena's legal team, meanwhile, worked tirelessly to tie up the investigations in red tape. Lawsuits were filed, counterclaims were made, and any journalist who published stories about her found themselves mired in legal battles that drained their time and resources. Elena knew that she couldn't stop the investigations entirely, but she could slow them down and make them so costly that many would simply give up.

But even as she fought back, Elena knew that she was losing control. The more desperate her actions became, the more attention she attracted. The public was starting to see through the facade, recognizing her attempts to manipulate the narrative for what they were. And while some still admired her for her power and determination, others saw her as a symbol of corruption—someone who would do anything to protect herself, no matter the cost.

In her luxurious office, Elena sat alone, gazing out at the city skyline. She had once taken great pride in her view—the sprawling city below, filled with people who admired her success, who aspired to be like her. Now, that same view felt cold and distant, a reminder of how far she had fallen.

Her empire, once invincible, was teetering on the edge of collapse. The investigations were closing in, and no matter how many legal maneuvers she tried, no matter how many threats she made, she couldn't stop the inevitable. The media had turned against her, and the public no longer saw her as a successful businesswoman—they saw her as a ruthless tyrant, willing to destroy anyone who got in her way.

Elena still had her wealth, her power, and her connections. But as she sat there, alone in her office, she realized that all of it was slipping away. Her paranoia had driven away the people she had once relied on, and the ruthlessness that had served her so well in the past was now destroying her from within.

The fight for control had consumed her, and in the process, she had lost everything that truly mattered. Elena Marcetti was still the Queen of Piracy, but her reign was coming to an end. And as the investigations closed in, she couldn't help but wonder: was this the price she had to pay for the empire she had built?

Elena's struggle to maintain control had only driven her empire closer to collapse. Her desperation, her paranoia, and her ruthlessness had alienated those who might have helped her, leaving her isolated at the top. And as the investigations continued to close in, it became clear that Elena's time as the Queen of Piracy was running out.

The question that remained was no longer whether Elena would fall—but how far she would drag others down with her when she did.

# Chapter 15: A House of Cards

Elena Marcetti had always prided herself on the stability and strength of the empire she had built. For years, she had ruled her world with absolute authority, crafting a business empire that combined legitimate enterprises with illegal dealings. Her reputation had been untouchable, her power unrivaled. But now, it seemed that the foundation she had built was nothing more than a fragile house of cards, one that was beginning to collapse in on itself.

Everything was unraveling—faster than even she had anticipated. The media had exposed cracks in her empire, the authorities were closing in, and the public, once enamored by her success, had turned against her. Now, with each passing day, Elena watched helplessly as her once-loyal followers began to desert her, and her carefully constructed empire crumbled around her.

**It started with whispers in the boardrooms and among her top executives. Elena had always known that the people around her weren't truly loyal; they were loyal to the power and wealth she represented. But as the pressure mounted, those same people began looking for exits, fearing they would be caught in the wreckage of her downfall.**

One morning, as Elena walked into her high-rise office, the atmosphere was different. Usually, the corridors buzzed with energy and efficiency, filled with employees eager to execute her orders. But now, there was a palpable sense of dread. People avoided eye contact, whispered in corners, and the once-lively office seemed eerily quiet. Elena's sharp instincts told her that something was wrong.

Her fears were confirmed later that day when her chief financial officer, a man who had been with her for nearly a decade, abruptly resigned. His resignation letter was brief and cold, citing "personal reasons," but Elena knew the truth. He was jumping ship, like so many others were preparing to do.

Not long after, her head of legal—a critical figure who had helped navigate the grey areas of her business dealings—also handed in her resignation. This hit Elena hard. The legal team had always been her shield, protecting her from the prying eyes of law enforcement, but now, even they were abandoning her.

Elena's empire was crumbling from the inside, and the cracks were spreading faster than she could contain.

Outside her inner circle, the repercussions of the investigations and negative press were spreading like wildfire. Her suppliers—those who had long relied on Elena's power and influence—began to distance themselves from her empire. Elena had always maintained a firm grip on her suppliers, using both her financial leverage and, when necessary, intimidation to keep them in line. But now, with law enforcement scrutinizing every aspect of her operations, those suppliers were no longer willing to take the risk of doing business with her.

One by one, they began to pull out of contracts, citing "legal concerns" and "unforeseen circumstances." Elena received emails and phone calls from suppliers who had once been loyal, informing her that they could no longer do business with her. Some of them were blunt, stating outright that they didn't want to be associated with her as the media frenzy grew. Others were more cautious, offering vague excuses, but the message was clear—her network of suppliers was collapsing.

This was a devastating blow to her empire. Without a reliable supply chain, Elena's business couldn't function. Her illegal operations relied heavily on the cooperation of those suppliers to move counterfeit goods, and without them, entire parts of her empire ground to a halt. Orders went unfulfilled, shipments were delayed, and her customers began to lose faith in her ability to deliver.

Worse still, some of her competitors—sensing her vulnerability—swooped in to take advantage. They offered her suppliers better deals, promising them stability and protection, something Elena could no longer guarantee. In a matter of weeks, many of her key suppliers had switched allegiances, leaving her scrambling to find replacements in an increasingly hostile market.

As if the abandonment of her suppliers wasn't bad enough, Elena faced a new wave of challenges as law enforcement ramped up their efforts to dismantle her empire. For months, the authorities had been investigating her operations, but now they were making their move. They had gathered enough evidence, and the arrests began.

The first to fall was her head of distribution. He was arrested at his home in the early hours of the morning, dragged out in handcuffs while his family looked on in shock. Elena heard about the arrest from a news report before she even had a chance to react. This man had been instrumental in the smooth operation of her global distribution network, ensuring that goods—both legal and illegal—flowed without interruption. His arrest was a significant blow to her organization, but it was only the beginning.

Within days, more of her top executives were arrested. The authorities had been building their case for months, quietly collecting evidence and waiting for the right moment to strike. Now, they were executing their plan with ruthless precision, taking down key figures in Elena's organization one by one.

Her offices were raided, and documents were seized. The authorities were no longer content with watching from the sidelines—they were actively dismantling her empire. Her legal team tried to fight back, filing motions to delay the investigations and suppress the evidence, but the momentum was against them. Elena knew that it was only a matter of time before the entire structure of her business collapsed.

As more of her executives were arrested, Elena's paranoia reached new heights. She had always been cautious, always kept a close eye on those around her, but now, she saw betrayal everywhere. The arrests were too targeted, too precise—it felt like someone from within her organization was feeding information to the authorities.

She conducted her own internal investigation, trying to root out the traitor, but the more she searched, the more she realized how deep the betrayal ran. People she had trusted for years were turning against her, either to save themselves or to strike a deal with the authorities.

One of her closest allies, a senior executive who had been by her side since the early days of her empire, was caught in a wiretap giving information to the authorities in exchange for immunity. Elena had always suspected that loyalty was a fragile thing, but the sting of this particular betrayal cut deeper than she expected. It wasn't just the loss of an ally—it was the realization that her once-loyal followers were now actively working to bring her down.

Elena took swift and decisive action, but the damage was done. She purged her inner circle of anyone she suspected of disloyalty, firing people left and right, but it was too late. The once-solid core of her empire was now fractured, and she could feel control slipping further and further from her grasp.

As the legal noose tightened around her, Elena faced another challenge: the court of public opinion. The media had been relentless in their coverage of her downfall, and the more they uncovered, the more the public turned against her. Elena had once been seen as a savvy businesswoman, a symbol of success and power. But now, the headlines painted a very different picture.

"Queen of Piracy Exposed," read one headline. "The Fall of Elena Marcetti," said another. The press delved into every aspect of her life, uncovering details about her shady dealings, her manipulation of the legal system, and her use of bribery and intimidation to maintain control. Her image was in tatters, and no amount of public relations could salvage it.

Elena tried to fight back, issuing statements through her PR team, claiming that she was being unfairly targeted by the media. But the public wasn't buying it. They had seen the headlines, watched the news reports, and read the exposés. Elena was no longer the respected figure she had once been—she was now a symbol of corruption, greed, and deception.

As public opinion turned against her, Elena found herself increasingly isolated. Business partners distanced themselves, investors withdrew their support, and even some of her political allies began to back away. Elena had always known that loyalty in business and politics was fleeting, but she hadn't expected the exodus to happen so quickly.

In the final days of her empire, Elena's once-loyal followers deserted her. Her employees, sensing that the end was near, began to resign in droves. Some of them were afraid of being caught up in the legal fallout, while others simply didn't want to be associated with a sinking ship.

Even her personal staff—people who had worked for her for years—began to leave. Her personal assistant, who had been by her side for over a decade, quit with little more than a brief note on her desk. Her security team, once fiercely loyal, began to leave as well, citing "personal reasons" but clearly not wanting to be involved in the inevitable collapse.

Elena's empire, once a thriving and powerful machine, had been reduced to a skeleton crew. The offices that had once buzzed with activity were now empty, and the few remaining employees were demoralized, working only because they had no other options. Elena's company was a shell of its former self, and there was little she could do to stop the bleeding.

In the end, Elena's empire collapsed not with a dramatic fall, but with a slow and painful disintegration. Her suppliers were gone, her key executives were either arrested or had fled, and her loyal followers had abandoned her. The legal cases against her were gaining momentum, and her financial reserves were being drained by the constant legal battles.

Elena watched helplessly as her empire crumbled, piece by piece. The once-mighty house of cards she had built was now nothing more than a pile of rubble, and there was no one left to help her rebuild it.

For years, she had ruled with an iron fist, using power, fear, and manipulation to maintain control. But in the end, it was those very same tools that had led to her downfall. The empire she had worked so hard to build had collapsed, and Elena Marcetti, the Queen of Piracy, was left standing alone in the ruins.

# Chapter 16: The Fall

Elena Marcetti stood in the vast, silent emptiness of her once-bustling headquarters. The air felt heavier, almost suffocating, as though the walls themselves were pressing in, whispering the tales of deceit, manipulation, and ambition that had once fueled her empire. This was the end. She had built an empire that spanned continents, controlled markets, and, at its peak, had made her one of the most feared and revered figures in the corporate world. But now, her empire was nothing but ashes, and all that remained was the inevitable fall from grace.

The journey to the top had been relentless, and the descent, while equally swift, was even more painful. Elena's name, once synonymous with power and success, was now forever linked to corruption, betrayal, and corporate greed. As the world watched her empire crumble, the full extent of her illegal operations began to unravel before the eyes of the public. And at the heart of this downfall, Elena found herself betrayed not by enemies or rivals—but by those she had trusted the most.

**As law enforcement agencies delved deeper into her illegal operations, Elena was faced with the harsh truth: her closest confidants, people she had trusted with the most delicate aspects of her empire, had turned on her. It began with whispers, rumors that some of her inner circle were cooperating with the authorities. Elena had always kept a tight leash on her people, ensuring that loyalty was rewarded and betrayal was dealt with ruthlessly. But in the face of mounting legal pressure, those once-loyal allies were now looking to save themselves.**

One of the first betrayals came from someone Elena never expected—Maria, her chief operations officer. Maria had been with

Elena since the early days of her business, overseeing the expansion of her empire into new territories and ensuring that both her legal and illegal operations ran smoothly. Elena had trusted her with everything, believing that Maria's ambition matched her own. But as the authorities zeroed in on the web of counterfeit goods that spanned continents, Maria saw an opportunity to cut a deal.

Elena received the news of Maria's betrayal from her lawyer during a late-night meeting. Maria had provided crucial evidence to the investigators—evidence that not only detailed the scope of Elena's counterfeit operations but also implicated her in money laundering, tax evasion, and bribery schemes that extended far beyond what Elena had anticipated.

"She's testified against you," her lawyer said quietly, avoiding Elena's gaze. "She's given them everything."

Elena's hands tightened into fists as the weight of the betrayal sank in. Maria had been more than just an employee—she had been a partner in crime, someone Elena had groomed to be her second-in-command. And now, in the face of her empire's collapse, Maria had chosen to save herself, leaving Elena to bear the brunt of the legal onslaught.

With Maria's testimony, the investigations into Elena's empire accelerated. What had once been whispers and speculation in the press was now confirmed by hard evidence. The world began to learn about the massive web of counterfeit goods that Elena had built over the years, a network that stretched across continents and infiltrated multiple industries. From luxury fashion to pharmaceuticals, electronics, and even food products, Elena's empire had been responsible for flooding markets with counterfeit goods, raking in billions in profits while undermining legitimate businesses and endangering consumers.

The revelations shocked the public. People had known that Elena was a powerful businesswoman, but the scale of her illegal operations was far greater than anyone had imagined. News outlets ran exposés detailing how Elena's empire had exploited loopholes in international trade laws, bribed customs officials, and used shell companies to move counterfeit goods across borders undetected. Journalists dug deep into her past, uncovering years of shady deals, questionable partnerships, and ruthless tactics that had allowed her to maintain her dominance in the global market.

The media frenzy only intensified as more details emerged. Elena's name became synonymous with corporate greed and deception. Documentaries were made, investigative reports aired, and her face appeared on the covers of magazines and newspapers with headlines that declared the fall of "The Queen of Counterfeit."

But the media's scrutiny was only one aspect of her downfall. The government had taken notice, and they were moving swiftly to dismantle her empire for good.

Once the full extent of Elena's illegal operations was uncovered, the government wasted no time in taking action. Multiple agencies, including the FBI, Interpol, and financial crime units, launched coordinated efforts to seize her assets and bring her to justice. The sheer scope of her empire had allowed her to evade the law for years, but now, with her closest allies betraying her and the media exposing her every move, there was nowhere left for her to hide.

One morning, Elena woke to the sound of her doorbell ringing. As she opened the door, she was met by a team of government agents, armed with search warrants and court orders. They had come to seize her property—her luxury cars, her penthouse, her art collection, and even her private jet. All of it was being taken as part of the government's efforts to recover the billions she had amassed through illegal means.

Elena watched as the agents moved through her home, cataloguing every item of value. Her lawyer had warned her that this day would come, but seeing it unfold before her eyes was a different kind of pain. This wasn't just about losing material possessions; it was about losing the identity she had built over decades. Elena Marcetti, the woman who had once controlled an empire, was now watching it all slip away, piece by piece.

As her assets were seized, the government also froze her bank accounts, cutting off her access to the wealth she had once taken for granted. Elena's financial empire, built on a mix of legitimate and illegitimate ventures, was being dismantled. Her offshore accounts, carefully hidden through a maze of shell companies and trusts, were exposed and drained. The money that had once flowed so freely was now being clawed back by authorities.

The legal actions against Elena weren't just about seizing her assets. The government wanted to make an example of her, to show the world that no one was above the law. As the investigations continued, Elena found herself facing multiple criminal charges, including racketeering, money laundering, tax evasion, and fraud. The prosecutors were determined to bring her down, and they had the evidence to do it.

The trials that followed were highly publicized, with reporters and cameras camped outside the courthouse each day, eager for any glimpse of the disgraced businesswoman. Elena, once used to commanding rooms with her presence, now found herself sitting in courtrooms, surrounded by lawyers and journalists, as prosecutors laid out the full extent of her crimes.

Witnesses were called to testify against her, including former employees, business partners, and even some of her closest confidants. They detailed the inner workings of her empire, exposing the lengths she had gone to in order to evade the law and maintain her control over the counterfeit market. Each testimony was another blow to Elena's reputation, another crack in the facade she had worked so hard to build.

The public, once intrigued by her success, had turned against her completely. Social media was flooded with outrage, with people calling for her to be held accountable for the damage she had caused. The image of Elena Marcetti, once the powerful and glamorous "Queen of Piracy," was now that of a criminal mastermind, a symbol of everything that was wrong with corporate greed.

As the legal battles dragged on, Elena's empire continued to collapse. The companies she had built, both legitimate and illegitimate, were either sold off or shut down. Her once-loyal executives, many of whom had been arrested or fled the country, were no longer there to manage the day-to-day operations. Without its leader, the empire that had once dominated markets around the world was falling apart.

Her remaining businesses, struggling to distance themselves from the scandal, were forced to lay off employees and restructure. Investors, fearing further legal repercussions, withdrew their support, leaving many of her companies bankrupt. Suppliers and partners, once eager to do business with her, now shunned her, unwilling to be associated with the growing scandal.

Even her personal relationships suffered. Friends and acquaintances, many of whom had benefited from her success, distanced themselves as her legal troubles mounted. Elena had always been a solitary figure, preferring power and control over personal connections, but now, in the face of her downfall, she realized just how alone she truly was.

As the dust settled, it became clear that Elena Marcetti's name would forever be tarnished. What had once been a symbol of success and ambition was now a cautionary tale of corporate greed, deception, and hubris. Her empire, once a towering force in the global market, had been reduced to rubble, and Elena herself was facing the possibility of spending the rest of her life in prison.

In the end, Elena had no one to blame but herself. She had built her empire on lies, manipulation, and the exploitation of others, and now, those very same tactics had led to her downfall. The people she had trusted had turned against her, the government had seized everything she owned, and the public had branded her a criminal.

Elena Marcetti, the once-powerful queen, had fallen from her throne, and the world would never forget her downfall.

# Chapter 17: Escape or Capture?

The early morning light filtered through the windows of Elena Marcetti's penthouse, casting long shadows across the sleek, minimalistic furniture that filled the space. But despite the outward serenity of her surroundings, the tension in the air was palpable. Elena paced the floor, her mind racing as the pieces of her once-mighty empire lay scattered around her, irreparable. It was no longer just a matter of preserving her reputation or salvaging her fortune. This was about survival.

The noose was tightening. Law enforcement had closed in on every front, dismantling what remained of her empire, arresting her lieutenants, freezing her assets, and raiding her properties. Her lawyer had warned her—there was no escaping the inevitable. With the overwhelming evidence against her, it was only a matter of days, maybe hours, before the authorities came knocking on her door to arrest her for good.

But Elena Marcetti had never been one to surrender without a fight. As everything around her collapsed, she began to consider the unthinkable: disappearing, vanishing without a trace, before they could bring her to justice.

**Elena had always prided herself on being two steps ahead of everyone else, and this situation was no different. Over the years, she had quietly prepared for a day like this. In her line of work, the prospect of being hunted down by authorities or betrayed by associates was always looming. She had learned from the fates of other powerful figures who had been brought down by their own ambitions or bad luck. Elena knew better than to leave her fate in the hands of others.**

She had long ago set up contingencies—a network of offshore accounts, false identities, and safe houses scattered across the globe. Her counterfeit operations had taught her how to forge documents, evade surveillance, and exploit legal loopholes. Now, all of these skills would serve her well in her greatest and most dangerous challenge: escaping capture.

Elena pulled out her encrypted phone and dialed a number she hadn't called in years. It rang once before a voice on the other end answered with a simple, "It's time?"

"Yes," Elena replied. "I need the extraction. Today."

Her voice was cold, controlled, despite the storm swirling around her. This was her last card to play, and it had to be perfect. The plan was simple on paper but required flawless execution: she would fake her disappearance and flee the country using one of her false identities, taking with her what little remained of her liquid assets. She had prepped for this moment years ago, and now, with the authorities closing in, it was her only option.

Elena had never been sentimental, but as she looked around her penthouse one last time, she felt a pang of loss. This had been her world, her sanctuary, a symbol of her power and success. She had built everything from nothing, rising from a scrappy entrepreneur to a feared and respected mogul. Now, she had to leave it all behind.

She walked over to the desk in the corner of the room, where a sleek black suitcase sat. Inside were the essentials: several passports under different aliases, enough cash to survive for months, a few pieces of her most valuable jewelry, and a burner phone. She had also secured access to a hidden stash of funds in an offshore account, the last remnants of her fortune that the government hadn't been able to freeze.

As Elena closed the suitcase and zipped it shut, she took a deep breath. There would be no time for hesitation. Every second counted. The plan was set in motion—her car was waiting for her in the basement garage, and a private jet had been arranged to take her to a country with no extradition treaty. But before she left, there was one more loose end to tie up.

She picked up her personal phone and dialed another number. This time, it was a familiar voice that answered—Alberto, her last remaining confidant, and one of the few people who had stuck by her through the collapse of her empire. He was the only person she trusted enough to know about her plan.

"I'm leaving," she said without preamble.

"Are you sure?" Alberto's voice was tense. "The authorities are everywhere. It's a huge risk."

"I don't have a choice," Elena replied. "If I stay, they'll arrest me within days. I won't go down like that."

There was a pause on the other end of the line before Alberto spoke again. "Be careful, Elena. They're watching everything."

"I know," she said softly. "Thank you, Alberto. For everything."

And with that, she hung up, knowing that this might be the last time she ever spoke to him.

The first phase of the escape plan began as soon as Elena left her penthouse. She took the private elevator down to the basement garage, where a sleek, nondescript black car awaited her. Her driver was already inside, engine running, ready to whisk her away to the next step of the plan. Elena slid into the backseat, pulling her sunglasses over her eyes as the car glided out of the building and into the bustling city streets.

Elena's heart raced as they sped through the city. Every red light, every intersection, every turn could bring her closer to capture. She couldn't help but glance nervously out of the window, scanning the streets for signs of surveillance. But so far, nothing seemed out of the ordinary. The authorities hadn't caught wind of her plan yet, but they were closing in fast.

Her destination was a private airstrip on the outskirts of the city. There, a jet waited to take her to a remote country where extradition would be nearly impossible. The country she had chosen was obscure, politically unstable, but with the right connections—connections she had cultivated over the years—she would be able to blend in, rebuild her life under a new identity.

As the car approached the airstrip, Elena felt a slight sense of relief. She could see the jet in the distance, its engines already running. The driver pulled up to the edge of the tarmac, and Elena stepped out, suitcase in hand, walking briskly towards the plane.

But just as she was about to reach the jet, her phone buzzed. It was a text message—an encrypted one from one of her contacts within law enforcement. It read: "They know."

Panic surged through Elena's veins. Her breath quickened as she glanced around, her eyes scanning the empty tarmac. Was this a trap? Had the authorities been waiting for her all along? Her heart pounded as she considered her options. Should she board the jet and risk it, or should she abandon the plan and run?

Before she could make a decision, she saw them—two black SUVs barreling down the road towards the airstrip. It was too late. They had found her.

Without hesitation, Elena turned on her heels and ran back towards the car, her mind racing for an escape route. Her driver, sensing the danger, revved the engine and sped towards her. The jet was no longer an option—she had to disappear now, on foot if necessary.

Elena jumped into the car just as the black SUVs screeched to a halt a few hundred feet away. The authorities were close, but not close enough. Her driver floored the gas pedal, the car roaring to life as it sped away from the airstrip, tires squealing. The chase was on.

Elena gripped the seat as the car swerved through the narrow streets, weaving between traffic, trying to put as much distance between them and the pursuing vehicles as possible. Her mind raced, trying to figure out her next move. She couldn't go to the jet, and the authorities would be searching every inch of the city for her. She needed to disappear, now.

As they sped through the city, Elena's driver took a sharp turn down a narrow alley, slowing down as they approached a nondescript building. It was a safe house, one of the many Elena had prepared for situations like this. She had hoped never to use it, but now it was her only option.

They pulled into the underground garage, and Elena jumped out, her suitcase in hand. She hurried inside, her heart pounding, as the door to the garage closed behind her. For now, she was safe. But she knew it was only a matter of time before the authorities tracked her down.

Inside the safe house, Elena took a deep breath, trying to calm her racing heart. She had managed to evade capture, but for how long? She knew that law enforcement was relentless, and they wouldn't stop until they had her in custody. The next phase of her escape had to be executed flawlessly.

She sat down at the small, unremarkable desk in the corner of the room and opened her suitcase. Inside, alongside the cash and passports, was a slim, encrypted laptop. Elena powered it on, accessing a secure network that connected her to a vast web of contacts around the world. She needed to vanish completely, erasing every trace of her existence.

Her plan was already in motion. Within hours, her digital footprint would disappear—bank accounts drained, phone records wiped, and every trace of her online presence erased. Elena had spent years building false identities, and now she would become one of them. She would become someone else entirely.

Her next move was to leave the city entirely, under the radar. She wouldn't make the mistake of using commercial transportation or private jets again. Instead, she would travel across the border by land, using one of the many underground smuggling routes she had helped establish during her empire's expansion. It was risky, but it was her only option.

As Elena vanished into the shadows, the world was left in a state of shock and speculation. News of her sudden disappearance spread like wildfire, dominating headlines and social media. The public was enthralled by the mystery of Elena Marcetti—once a powerful figure at the top of her game, now a fugitive on the run.

Rumors swirled about her fate. Some believed she had fled the country and was living in luxury somewhere in South America or Europe. Others thought she had gone underground, living in constant fear of capture. There were even conspiracy theories suggesting that she had faked her own death to escape justice.

But no one knew for sure. Not her enemies, not her allies, and certainly not the authorities. Elena had vanished without a trace, leaving behind nothing but questions.

Days turned into weeks, and the hunt for Elena intensified. Law enforcement agencies from multiple countries were involved, scouring every lead, every tip, in an effort to track her down. But Elena had been careful—her tracks were covered, her digital footprint erased. She had disappeared into thin air.

But even as the world continued to search for her, Elena knew that she could never fully relax. The life of a fugitive was one of constant vigilance, always looking over her shoulder, never trusting anyone. She had escaped capture, but at what cost?

As she sat in her latest safe house, somewhere in a remote part of the world, Elena stared out of the window, lost in thought. She had won—for now. But she knew the truth: the chase was far from over. And in the end, no matter how far she ran or how carefully she hid, the past always had a way of catching up.

Would she escape forever, or would she one day face the justice she had evaded for so long?

Only time would tell.

# Chapter 18: The Aftermath

The collapse of Elena Marcetti's empire sent shockwaves around the world. What had started as whispers of corruption and deceit soon grew into a global scandal, shaking the foundations of businesses, governments, and markets alike. The extent of Elena's operations had been far more vast and complex than anyone had imagined. As the dust settled, the full impact of her counterfeit empire came to light, and the fallout was devastating.

In boardrooms and offices across continents, nervous executives reviewed contracts and supply chains, desperately trying to distance themselves from the tangled web that Elena had woven. For years, her counterfeit goods had infiltrated legitimate businesses, from high-end fashion to everyday consumer products. And now that her empire had crumbled, those who had unwittingly played a part in it were facing the consequences.

**As law enforcement agencies in multiple countries worked together to investigate the collapse of Elena's empire, they quickly realized that they were dealing with one of the most sophisticated operations they had ever encountered. Elena's network of counterfeit goods spanned continents, involving thousands of people, businesses, and shell companies. From luxury handbags to electronics, pharmaceuticals, and even automotive parts, Elena's empire had touched every corner of the global market.**

Investigators were stunned by the complexity of the system Elena had built. She had created a vast network of factories, distributors, and middlemen, all working under layers of false identities and shadow corporations. Many of these companies had been set up in countries with lax regulations, making it difficult for authorities to trace the origins of the counterfeit goods. Elena had exploited legal loopholes, taking advantage of the globalized economy to hide her operations in plain sight.

At the heart of her empire was a web of deception that had fooled even the most seasoned business leaders. Many companies had unknowingly sold Elena's counterfeit goods, believing they were dealing with legitimate suppliers. As the investigation unfolded, it became clear that some businesses had been duped for years, while others had turned a blind eye, preferring to ignore the suspiciously low prices for goods they knew should have cost much more.

The fallout was swift. Some of the biggest names in retail and manufacturing were forced to admit their ties to Elena's network, and many companies faced lawsuits from investors and customers who had been defrauded. The scandal triggered a wave of bankruptcies as businesses collapsed under the weight of their involvement in the counterfeit scheme. In a matter of months, the once-booming industries that had relied on Elena's goods were in ruins.

For the thousands of workers and employees whose jobs had depended on businesses tied to Elena's network, the collapse of her empire was catastrophic. Factories shut down overnight, leaving entire communities without income. Retailers, both small and large, were forced to close their doors, unable to recover from the financial losses caused by the counterfeit scandal.

In one small town in Eastern Europe, a textile factory that had unknowingly produced counterfeit luxury goods was shuttered, leaving hundreds of workers jobless. Many of these workers had no idea that they had been part of a global criminal enterprise. They had simply been doing their jobs, unaware that the fabrics they were handling were being used to create fake designer clothing. Now, they faced an uncertain future, with few options for employment in their economically struggling region.

Similar stories played out in countries around the world. From Asia to South America, entire supply chains crumbled as the ripple effects of Elena's empire collapse spread. The counterfeit goods had been cheap, but the cost to human lives was immeasurable. In many cases, workers in developing countries had been exploited, paid meager wages to produce goods that were sold at a fraction of the cost of the real thing.

For the investors who had poured their money into companies linked to Elena's network, the collapse was equally devastating. In some cases, people lost their life savings as stocks plummeted and businesses went bankrupt. Pension funds, hedge funds, and even individual retirement accounts had been invested in companies that, unbeknownst to them, had been profiting from the sale of counterfeit goods. Now, those investments were worthless, and the financial ruin was widespread.

As the investigation into Elena's empire deepened, it became clear that the scandal wasn't just limited to the business world. Politicians and government officials who had been linked to Elena's network were thrust into the spotlight, their careers hanging in the balance. Some had knowingly accepted bribes or turned a blind eye to Elena's illegal operations in exchange for campaign donations or business deals. Others had been caught in the web unwittingly, their political futures now at risk due to their associations with Elena's empire.

In several countries, high-ranking politicians faced charges of corruption and collusion. One particularly damning case involved a prominent senator in the United States who had received millions in donations from a company that had been one of Elena's biggest clients. The senator had publicly supported trade policies that made it easier for counterfeit goods to flow into the country, all while receiving financial support from businesses tied to Elena's network.

The scandal also exposed weaknesses in regulatory systems around the world. In many cases, governments had failed to properly regulate the flow of goods across borders, allowing counterfeit products to enter the market unchecked. Investigations revealed that customs officials in several countries had been paid off to ignore suspicious shipments, while others simply lacked the resources to identify counterfeit goods among the millions of legitimate products passing through their ports each day.

The political fallout was immense. In some countries, entire administrations were brought down by the scandal, as opposition parties seized on the opportunity to expose corruption and incompetence. Governments that had once prided themselves on their strong economies now faced public outrage as the extent of the counterfeit operations became known. The scandal became a rallying cry for reform, with voters demanding stricter regulations and greater transparency in the business world.

As the investigation into Elena's empire continued, one question remained on everyone's mind: Where was Elena Marcetti?

Her sudden disappearance had left law enforcement agencies around the world scrambling to track her down. With her vast resources and network of contacts, Elena had managed to evade capture for weeks, and no one knew where she was hiding. Rumors swirled that she had fled to a remote island in the Pacific, or that she was living under a new identity in South America. Others believed she had used her connections to escape to a country with no extradition treaty, where she could live out the rest of her days in luxury.

Interpol, the FBI, and other law enforcement agencies launched a global manhunt for Elena, but she had vanished without a trace. Despite their best efforts, the trail had gone cold. Every lead they followed turned out to be a dead end, and every associate they questioned claimed to have no knowledge of her whereabouts.

The public, too, was captivated by the mystery of Elena's disappearance. Media outlets ran stories speculating about her fate, with some even suggesting that she had faked her own death to avoid capture. Social media was flooded with conspiracy theories, with amateur sleuths combing through the details of her life in an attempt to solve the mystery. But no one could say for sure where she had gone.

Despite the global manhunt, Elena remained elusive, and her escape only added to her myth. In the eyes of the public, she became a larger-than-life figure—a master manipulator who had outsmarted the world and disappeared into the shadows.

In the wake of Elena's empire collapse, businesses and governments were left with the monumental task of rebuilding trust. The scandal had shattered consumer confidence, as people began to question the authenticity of the products they bought and the companies they supported. The counterfeit goods had infiltrated every level of the market, and now, consumers were left wondering if they had been unknowingly complicit in supporting a criminal enterprise.

Companies that had been linked to Elena's network faced an uphill battle in regaining the trust of their customers. Many launched internal investigations, firing executives and overhauling their supply chains in an attempt to distance themselves from the scandal. Others rebranded entirely, hoping to shed the taint of their association with Elena's counterfeit goods.

Governments, too, took action. In the United States, Europe, and Asia, new regulations were introduced to crack down on the sale of counterfeit goods and tighten control over international trade. Customs agencies received additional funding and resources to better identify and intercept counterfeit products at the border. Lawmakers pushed for greater transparency in supply chains, requiring companies to disclose the origins of their products and verify the legitimacy of their suppliers.

But despite these efforts, the damage had been done. The global economy had taken a massive hit, and the road to recovery would be long and difficult. The scandal had exposed the dark side of globalization, where unchecked greed and corruption had allowed a criminal empire to flourish for years, hidden in plain sight.

As the world grappled with the aftermath of Elena's empire collapse, one thing became clear: the scandal had been a wake-up call for businesses, governments, and consumers alike. It had exposed the vulnerabilities of the global economy and highlighted the need for greater accountability and oversight.

For businesses, the lesson was simple: trust, but verify. Companies could no longer afford to rely on blind faith in their suppliers. Due diligence, transparency, and ethical sourcing would become the new standard, as businesses sought to protect themselves from future scandals.

For governments, the collapse of Elena's empire underscored the need for stronger regulations and international cooperation. The counterfeit goods trade had flourished in the gaps between regulatory frameworks, and only by working together could countries hope to prevent future criminal enterprises from taking root.

For consumers, the scandal was a reminder that the choices they made had consequences. The allure of cheap goods often came at a hidden cost, and the counterfeit trade had real-world implications for workers, businesses, and economies around the world.

In the end, the collapse of Elena Marcetti's empire marked the end of an era. For years, she had operated in the shadows, building a global network of counterfeit goods that had infiltrated every corner of the market. But her empire had crumbled, and now the world was left to pick up the pieces.

Elena had disappeared, her fate unknown. But the legacy of her empire lived on—a cautionary tale of greed, deception, and the far-reaching consequences of unchecked ambition. The world would never forget the name Elena Marcetti, and the lessons learned from her empire's collapse would shape the future of global trade for years to come.

# Chapter 19: Where is She?

In the wake of the downfall of Elena Marcetti's empire, the world buzzed with speculation about her fate. As news outlets reported daily on the aftermath of her colossal fraud, whispers of her possible escape spread like wildfire. Some claimed she had fled to a remote island, where the azure waters would hide her from the prying eyes of law enforcement. Others believed she was living under an assumed identity in a bustling city, blending in with the everyday crowd. The mystery surrounding her disappearance only deepened with each passing day.

Across social media platforms, amateur sleuths and conspiracy theorists fervently debated Elena's fate. A thread on a popular online forum garnered thousands of comments, as users shared their theories and speculated on her next moves. Some claimed to have found her footprints in the sands of a small island in the Caribbean, while others suggested she had vanished into the mountains of South America, where she could live off the grid.

"Elena is too smart to just disappear without a plan," one user wrote. "She could be in a country with no extradition treaty, perhaps somewhere in Southeast Asia. If she has the right contacts, she could easily establish a new life."

Another user countered, "Or she could be right under our noses. With the right disguise and a little cash, she could easily blend in anywhere. Think about it: she built an empire by manipulating perceptions—why not do the same now?"

The media fed into this frenzy, with sensational headlines and stories. "Where is the Queen of Piracy?" asked one tabloid, while another proclaimed, "Elena Marcetti: The Great Escape!" The allure of her enigmatic character turned her into a legend, an almost mythical figure whose cunning and intelligence had allowed her to elude the authorities.

Meanwhile, television shows began to air episodes dedicated to her life and disappearance, presenting Elena as a modern-day Robin Hood—albeit one who had walked the fine line between legality and criminality. Documentaries highlighted her rise to power, showcasing her charisma, sharp mind, and ruthless ambition. They painted a picture of a woman who had captivated the world with her charm while building an empire based on deception.

As the investigation continued, law enforcement agencies from different countries joined forces to locate Elena. Interpol circulated alerts, and wanted posters featuring her image were plastered on billboards and kiosks in airports, train stations, and bus depots worldwide. The FBI, along with various international law enforcement agencies, formed task forces specifically dedicated to tracking her down.

Detectives poured over every lead, every sighting, and every piece of information that came their way. They examined surveillance footage from airports, border crossings, and ports, hoping to catch a glimpse of Elena. Each time a potential sighting was reported, the investigators would leap into action, but each time, they came up empty-handed.

In a dimly lit office in the heart of New York City, Agent Samantha Chen sat at her desk, surrounded by photographs of Elena and her known associates. "We need to broaden our search," she suggested during a meeting with her colleagues. "Elena is cunning. She may be hiding in plain sight, using her connections to live under the radar."

The task force launched a campaign to gather information from Elena's past associates, family, and acquaintances. They interviewed former employees, suppliers, and even old friends, trying to piece together the puzzle of her disappearance. But as they dug deeper, they found that many of those close to her were either too scared to talk or had vanished themselves.

The more they searched, the more elusive she became. One lead pointed to a sighting in Mexico, while another claimed she had been seen in a café in Paris. As investigators pursued each thread, Elena slipped further from their grasp, seemingly two steps ahead at every turn.

As time passed, Elena's disappearance took on a life of its own. Stories circulated about her cleverness and resourcefulness. She became a figure of fascination, almost a folk hero in the eyes of some. There were tales of her sitting on a beach somewhere, sipping cocktails and watching the world go by, a ghost of the empire she once ruled.

"Have you heard the latest?" a barista told a customer at a café in London. "They say she's living in a mansion on some hidden island, surrounded by luxury. Others say she's operating a new empire, but this time, it's all above board."

With every tale spun, her legend grew. Some even suggested she had taken on a new identity entirely, reinventing herself as a philanthropist or a businesswoman dedicated to social justice. As the days turned into weeks, and the weeks into months, the stories became more extravagant, and the public's fascination deepened.

In the world of social media influencers, memes began to emerge, depicting Elena as a glamorous figure on the run. Photoshopped images showed her lounging by pools, riding horses on beaches, and dining in exclusive restaurants. These playful representations only added to the allure, sparking conversations and debates among her followers.

"Could she really be this clever?" one user asked in a comment. "Or has she underestimated the law's resolve to find her?"

Despite the legends, the reality of the search was grim. The longer Elena remained missing, the more pressure mounted on law enforcement. Public outcry for justice grew, fueled by stories of the victims of her counterfeit goods empire—those who had lost their livelihoods and savings. Families were devastated, businesses were shuttered, and people were angry.

As the investigation dragged on, the task force faced criticism for their inability to locate her. Media outlets began to question their effectiveness, demanding answers and accountability. News segments aired featuring angry consumers and former employees, all eager to see justice served.

On a chilly November morning, Agent Chen addressed the press, her expression grave. "We are doing everything in our power to locate Elena Marcetti. We ask the public for their help—if you have any information, please come forward. No one is above the law, and we will not rest until we find her."

Despite her determination, Chen felt the weight of the world pressing down on her. Each passing day felt like a missed opportunity, and with each rumor of Elena's whereabouts, she could feel the case slipping further from her grasp.

The media frenzy continued to swirl around Elena's disappearance, and every so often, a new lead would catch fire, igniting public interest once more. "Breaking news!" a morning show host exclaimed one day, "Reports claim Elena Marcetti was spotted in a market in Bali!"

This led to a flurry of activity, with reporters and cameramen flocking to the location. However, as had happened before, the lead turned out to be a false alarm. The woman who had been mistaken for Elena was simply a local vendor with a striking resemblance.

Despite the setbacks, the media persisted. They constructed elaborate timelines, detailing Elena's rise and fall, intertwining her story with other high-profile cases of corporate fraud and white-collar crime. Each new development was scrutinized, dissected, and rehashed on television, and internet forums buzzed with speculation.

The phenomenon of "Elena Watch" became popular, with online groups forming to share updates and theories. Some even offered rewards for information leading to her capture, while others raised funds to create a documentary that would tell her story.

As her story continued to evolve, Elena became a symbol of the complexities of greed and ambition. She was no longer just a businesswoman; she represented the duality of human nature—brilliant yet flawed, driven yet deceptive.

Realizing that the investigation needed a new approach, the task force expanded their search internationally. They collaborated with law enforcement agencies from various countries, pooling resources, information, and expertise. Teams traveled to different continents, interviewing locals and tracking down leads that might have once seemed insignificant.

In Italy, a detective named Marco Rossi, who had studied Elena's case closely, believed she might return to her roots. He combed through records of real estate transactions, looking for any signs of her re-emergence. He visited small villages, cafes, and bars where Elena might be recognized. After weeks of investigation, he was convinced that she had slipped back into Italy, disguised as a local.

Meanwhile, in South America, another team focused on tracking down leads that suggested she might be financing operations for a new business venture. As they followed the money trail, they uncovered connections to shadowy figures in the criminal underworld. These revelations only fueled the urgency of the investigation, but they also complicated it further.

Despite the international efforts, the search remained fruitless. Each time the investigators felt they were closing in, Elena eluded them once again, slipping through their fingers like smoke.

As the months dragged on without a sign of Elena, the impact of her disappearance rippled through the world. While businesses sought to recover from the fallout of her empire, many found it challenging to regain consumer trust. New regulations and laws were enacted to prevent similar scams from occurring in the future, but for many, the damage was already done.

Victims of Elena's counterfeit empire still shared their stories, hoping to bring attention to their plight. Online petitions circulated, demanding justice and accountability from those who had turned a blind eye to the corruption. Grassroots movements sprang up, pushing for greater transparency in business practices and more stringent regulations on the import of goods.

As a result of the scandal, public awareness surrounding counterfeit goods increased significantly. Consumers became more vigilant, often researching products and brands before making purchases. Companies that had been accused of selling counterfeit goods invested in quality assurance and certification programs to reassure customers of their authenticity.

Elena's disappearance remained an open wound, a stark reminder of the dangers of unchecked ambition and greed. As the world tried to move forward, the shadow of her legacy lingered, shaping conversations around corporate responsibility and ethics.

In the quiet corners of the internet, Elena Marcetti transformed from a businesswoman into a legend. Blogs and vlogs chronicled her life and disappearance, blending fact with fiction. Young entrepreneurs idolized her for her audacity and ambition, seeing her as an emblem of what one could achieve, even if it meant breaking the rules.

As stories circulated, a darker narrative began to form. In bars and cafes, people whispered about her—some celebrated her cunning, while others loathed her deception. She became a topic of discussion among those who saw her as a cautionary tale of ambition gone awry.

In time, documentaries and books chronicling Elena's life emerged, each telling a different story. Some focused on her rise to power, while others delved into the ethics of her operations. Each perspective colored her legacy, creating a multifaceted figure who would forever be a part of the narrative surrounding corporate greed.

*As the investigation into her whereabouts continued, Elena Marcetti remained an enigma, her fate sealed in a shroud of mystery. Law enforcement was determined to uncover the truth, but as they chased shadows, they couldn't help but feel that the trail was growing colder.*

*For the world, Elena's story became a haunting legend—one that underscored the thin line between ambition and greed, and the lengths to which one might go to evade the consequences of their actions. The question lingered in the air: Where was she? And would she ever be found?*

*As authorities and citizens alike pondered these questions, the story of Elena Marcetti continued to evolve, reminding all that sometimes, the truth is stranger than fiction.*

# Chapter 20: Legacy of Shadows

Elena Marcetti's name echoed in boardrooms and cafes, whispered among entrepreneurs and students of business ethics alike. The world watched as her empire rose to dizzying heights and then plummeted into chaos, leaving a trail of confusion, anger, and loss in its wake. Although her physical presence had vanished, the shadow of her legacy lingered, a haunting reminder of the fine line between success and moral failure.

**Months after the collapse of Elena's counterfeit empire, the ripple effects continued to reverberate through global markets. The counterfeit goods she had proliferated—everything from luxury handbags to electronics—had not only undermined businesses but had also posed significant risks to consumers. Reports flooded in about defective products causing injuries, and many businesses that had unknowingly sold her goods faced bankruptcy, struggling to recover from the scandal that had rocked the industry.**

In a high-rise office in Manhattan, CEO Robert Kline surveyed the landscape of a once-thriving market now tainted by the shadow of deception. "How do we rebuild trust?" he pondered aloud during a meeting with his executive team. "This whole ordeal has left consumers skeptical about everything, including our brand."

His marketing director, Sarah, replied, "We need to focus on transparency. We should invest in campaigns that highlight our commitment to authenticity and ethical sourcing. We need to show consumers that we are different from Elena's empire."

Kline nodded, realizing that the road ahead would be long and difficult. Trust, once lost, was challenging to regain, and the damage done by Elena's actions was not easily erased. Companies across the globe began to realize that they could no longer afford to overlook their supply chains. They had to ensure that every product met the highest standards of quality and authenticity.

As businesses scrambled to repair their reputations, the moral questions surrounding Elena's empire became the subject of intense scrutiny. Was it solely her fault that counterfeit goods had infiltrated the market? Or did the entire system share responsibility?

Scholars and ethicists began to debate the nuances of corporate responsibility. "We need to look beyond Elena," said Dr. Marcus Hale, a prominent business ethics professor. "The problem isn't just her deception; it's the entire supply chain that allowed it to flourish. Businesses have to be more vigilant in ensuring the integrity of their products."

At universities, classes on business ethics saw a surge in enrollment. Students were eager to dissect Elena's methods and the systemic failures that had enabled her rise. Case studies began to circulate, exploring how companies could implement stronger ethical guidelines and how consumers could be more conscientious in their purchases.

In a lecture hall packed with eager students, Dr. Hale challenged his audience: "What role do you play as consumers? Are you complicit when you choose convenience over integrity?" His words struck a chord, leaving many students pondering their own purchasing habits. They began to realize that they could no longer view themselves as passive consumers; they had to take responsibility for the choices they made.

Despite the efforts of businesses and educators, the legacy of counterfeit goods remained a persistent issue in global markets. The allure of fake luxury items continued to attract consumers, especially among those who sought the prestige of high-end brands without the high price tag. Street vendors in major cities remained populated with counterfeit goods, and online marketplaces buzzed with listings for everything from fake designer clothes to knockoff electronics.

In Paris, a young woman named Camille scrolled through her social media feed, mesmerized by images of influencers flaunting the latest trends. "I can't believe I could never afford that," she thought, glancing at a photo of a coveted handbag. Her eyes drifted to an online ad for a near-identical replica at a fraction of the price.

"Why not?" she reasoned. "It looks the same." In that moment, the cycle continued, with consumers prioritizing aesthetics and status over authenticity. Elena's shadow loomed large in the form of a culture that celebrated imitation over innovation.

Meanwhile, authorities intensified their efforts to combat counterfeiting. Police raids on warehouses and shops selling counterfeit goods became more frequent, but it was a game of cat and mouse. For every batch of fake goods seized, another shipment would emerge from the shadows, often cleverly disguised as legitimate merchandise.

The personal stories of those affected by Elena's empire became increasingly poignant. Families who had invested in businesses that unknowingly sold her counterfeit goods faced financial ruin, their lives upended by a crisis they never saw coming.

At a community center in Chicago, a support group met to share their experiences. Among them was Jonathan, a small business owner who had lost everything when his shop was discovered to have sold counterfeit products. "I thought I was doing the right thing," he lamented, tears brimming in his eyes. "I never thought I'd be caught up in something so big."

Sitting next to him, Maria, a mother of two, shared her story. "I bought what I thought was a genuine product for my children. It was defective and nearly hurt them. I had no idea it was a fake. I just wanted to provide the best for my family."

The pain and frustration in the room were palpable as each person recounted their struggles. They were victims of Elena's greed, yet they also felt a profound sense of betrayal from the system that had failed to protect them.

In response to the widespread chaos, various organizations rallied to advocate for change. Consumer protection groups pushed for more stringent regulations on the sale of goods, while lawmakers proposed new legislation aimed at combating counterfeiting.

A congressional hearing was convened to discuss the fallout from Elena's empire and the need for reform. Politicians grilled witnesses, demanding answers about the systemic failures that had allowed counterfeiting to thrive. "How can we ensure that our markets remain safe for consumers?" asked Senator James Thompson, his voice resolute. "We cannot let another Elena Marcetti rise again."

As the hearing progressed, a call for transparency emerged. Lawmakers proposed initiatives that would require businesses to disclose their supply chains, ensuring that consumers could make informed choices about the products they purchased. The conversation shifted towards the importance of ethical manufacturing, with proponents emphasizing the need for a collaborative effort among businesses, governments, and consumers to create a safer marketplace.

As discussions surrounding corporate responsibility intensified, consumers began to recognize their power in shaping the marketplace. With social media as a tool for activism, they started to hold brands accountable for their practices. Hashtags like #BuyAuthentic and #EthicalConsumerism began trending, pushing businesses to adopt more ethical practices or risk losing their customer base.

In cafes and living rooms across the world, people engaged in conversations about the importance of supporting companies that prioritized authenticity. "It's not just about saving money; it's about supporting businesses that do things the right way," a young man named Leo explained to his friends as they discussed their shopping habits.

Consumers began to seek out information on brands before making purchases. Online forums buzzed with discussions about the merits of supporting ethical businesses over those with questionable practices. The culture of informed consumerism began to grow, and the narrative slowly shifted from one of blind consumption to one of conscious choice.

As Elena's story faded into the annals of history, her legacy posed questions that lingered in the minds of many. How far was one willing to go in the pursuit of success? What constituted ethical business practices? The line between ambition and moral failure was razor-thin, and the consequences of crossing it could be catastrophic.

In the hallowed halls of business schools, professors posed hypothetical scenarios to their students. "Imagine you are in Elena's shoes, facing immense pressure to succeed. What decisions would you make? How would you balance your ambition with your ethical responsibilities?"

The students grappled with these questions, their faces reflecting the tension of the moral dilemmas. Some argued that the pursuit of success could justify unethical actions, while others firmly believed that integrity should never be compromised, no matter the circumstances.

Through these discussions, the importance of ethical leadership began to resonate with the next generation of business leaders. They understood that true success was not merely defined by profits but by the impact they had on their communities, their employees, and the world at large.

In the aftermath of Elena's collapse, the world had a chance to reflect on the lessons learned. Businesses recognized the need for change, consumers embraced their power, and society began to re-evaluate its values. The echoes of Elena's choices served as a powerful reminder of the costs associated with unchecked ambition and the importance of moral integrity.

As the chapter of Elena Marcetti closed, it left behind a legacy of shadows—one that would influence future generations to tread carefully on the path of success. Her story had become a cautionary tale, a narrative woven into the fabric of business ethics that would inspire dialogue and reflection.

In a small cafe in Milan, a group of students engaged in a spirited discussion about ethical entrepreneurship. As they sipped their coffees, they pondered the future. "Let's make sure our legacy is one of integrity," one of them declared, setting the tone for the conversations that would continue long after Elena's name faded from headlines.

*Elena Marcetti may have vanished into the shadows, but the questions her story raised remained alive and relevant. The legacy of her empire, intertwined with the ongoing battle against counterfeiting, posed significant challenges and moral dilemmas for businesses and consumers alike.*

*As society moved forward, it carried with it the lessons learned from her rise and fall, striving to ensure that the line between success and moral failure would not be crossed again. And in doing so, the world began to embrace a new era—one characterized by accountability, transparency, and a commitment to ethical practices that honored the integrity of both businesses and consumers.*

*Elena's legacy, though shrouded in darkness, had the potential to illuminate the path toward a more responsible and ethical future for all.*

Dear Readers,

As I bring this journey to a close, I want to take a moment to express my heartfelt gratitude to each of you for joining me in exploring the rise and fall of Elena Marcetti. Her story—filled with ambition, deception, and moral dilemmas—has been a reflection of the complexities we face in our own lives and in the world of business today.

Writing this book was both a challenging and enlightening experience. It pushed me to confront difficult questions about ethics, responsibility, and the choices we make in pursuit of success. I hope that as you turned each page, you found yourself pondering not just the fate of Elena's empire but also the broader implications of our actions as consumers and leaders.

Elena's tale serves as a cautionary reminder of the thin line between ambition and moral failure. It is my hope that her legacy, although fraught with shadows, can inspire a new generation to embrace integrity and transparency in all their endeavors. In a world where counterfeit goods and corporate greed can so easily undermine trust, we must strive to build a marketplace grounded in ethical practices and a commitment to authenticity.

I encourage you to carry forward the lessons learned from this narrative. As consumers, let us choose to support businesses that prioritize ethical standards and transparency. As future leaders, let us commit to fostering environments that uphold integrity and accountability, ensuring that the legacy we leave behind is one of honor and respect.

Thank you for accompanying me on this journey through the complexities of human ambition and the quest for success. Your support means the world to me, and I look forward to hearing your thoughts and reflections on this story.

With deepest appreciation,
Smita Singh

# Don't miss out!

Visit the website below and you can sign up to receive emails whenever Smita Singh publishes a new book. There's no charge and no obligation.

https://books2read.com/r/B-A-LYEOB-KBKDF

BOOKS 2 READ

Connecting independent readers to independent writers.

Did you love *Shadows Of Commerce - The Queen of Piracy*? Then you should read *The Silent Hand: Behind the Market's Illusion*[1] by Smita Singh!

"The Silent Hand: Behind the Market's Illusion" is a story about stock market manipulation; it's a window into a world where the movements of a few can change the fate of many. It's a world where vast sums of money, hidden political ties, and the control of information dictate who wins and who loses—often leaving small traders holding the short end of the stick.

I was inspired to write this book after hearing stories from traders who had lost everything in market crashes that seemed to defy logic. As I dug deeper, I began to understand the extent of influence that big capital and political power have on markets. It's

---

1. https://books2read.com/u/bayJVa
2. https://books2read.com/u/bayJVa

a game designed to be unwinnable for the little guy, yet millions of people play it every day, unaware of the forces working against them.

This book follows the journey of Arjun, a journalist who stumbles upon this hidden world and embarks on a quest to expose the truth. Through his eyes, we'll see how a nexus of powerful individuals—the politicians, financiers, and media moguls—manipulate the market to serve their own interests, creating illusions that trap unsuspecting traders.

As you read Arjun's story, you might find yourself questioning whether such manipulation exists in the real world. The truth is, financial markets are far more complex than they appear. While the characters and events in this book are fictional, the mechanisms of manipulation they expose are very real.

I hope this story sheds light on the often invisible forces that shape our markets and inspires you to think critically about the narratives we're fed. The stock market, like many systems, is built on trust, but that trust can be easily broken when power and greed take the reins.

Milton Keynes UK
Ingram Content Group UK Ltd.
UKHW031144311024
450535UK00001B/21